By the same author

Ambush at North Platte
The River Flows West

Dead Man's Ra

The murder trail was eight years old when Jeff C
of Huntsville Prison and the only clue he had was
broken spur he had found that night beside Clint M
body.

Booth Anson's rambling Anvil range hemme
Merriweather ranch on all sides, but Clint's widow, A
stubbornly on. Anson had killed to build his empire –
dead man's range.

But a woman stood in his way now – would he balk at
woman? That was when Carmody picked up his gun.

Dead Man's Range

PAUL DURST

A Black Horse Western

ROBERT HALE · LONDON

© Paul Durst 1958
First published 1958
This edition published in Great Britain 2009

ISBN 978-0-7090-8791-5

Robert Hale Limited
Clerkenwell House
Clerkenwell Green
London EC1R 0HT

www.halebooks.com

Typeset by
Derek Doyle & Associates, Shaw Heath
Printed and bound in Great Britain by
CPI Antony Rowe, Chippenham and Eastbourne

CHAPTER 1

The train ground to a halt and a solitary passenger swung down to the platform. Dumping his warbag beside him he pulled a sack of tobacco from his shirt and gazed about him in the noonday heat. The man stood drawing idly on his cigarette, glancing up at the sign that read: SAND VALLEY. He hadn't noticed the train had gone, had no idea he had been standing there as long as he had. After eight years in prison a man has a strange sense of time.

He gazed beyond the depot toward the town. It had grown a little, but not much. He wondered if anybody here would remember him. Hardly likely. He had only been passing through when it happened and they sent him off to the state prison at Huntsville. Nobody would recognize him now, at twenty-eight, as the youngster he had been then. He found grim satisfaction in that. Picking up his warbag he crossed the depot platform and started up the single dusty street.

The heat lay heavy everywhere, even in the shade. He could even feel the heat of the dust as his boots sank into it. Sand Valley, Texas. Dust Valley would suit it better, he thought. He squinted his eyes against the glare and glanced beyond the length of the street.

A few assorted wagons were scattered along the street between an occasional tethered pony, and towards one of these a woman was leading a little girl of seven or eight followed by a scampering black and white puppy. The woman got into the buckboard and waited for the girl to follow with the pup. But the pup would not be caught, yipping playfully and dodging beneath the vehicle, ignoring the girl's cry of, 'Pinto, come *here*!'

Jeff Carmody lowered his warbag to the ground and stood watching. It was not the pup nor the girl that held his attention, but the woman. She was the first woman of his own age he had seen in eight years. The only woman, save two elderly ranchers' wives on the train. He felt a strange hollowness inside him at the sight of her. Her face was turned partly toward him as she watched the girl and the pup with an amused smile, but she had not seen him. He was glad of that, for it let him look his fill. He was sorry when the pup was caught at last and hoisted aboard and the buckboard clattered down the street.

Carmody gave a sigh and bent down to retrieve his warbag when a scream and a clatter brought him upright again. The buckboard had lost a wheel and had settled down on the rear axle, raising a cloud of dust as it dragged to a stop. The woman and the girl were stepping gingerly down from their tilting seat and glancing hopelessly at the wheel. The pup had tumbled to the ground and was now capering excitedly about, barking his enthusiasm.

In eight bitter years Carmody had forgotten how to smile. He was unaware that his offer of help sounded brusque and he wondered at the strange look the woman gave him when she accepted. He saw the woman was holding the hub nut out to him and noticed the wedding ring.

'This came off,' the woman was saying. 'I've got a wrench under the seat, but there's no jack. I'm afraid we'll have to unload before you can get it on. Those sacks of flour and things are pretty heavy.'

Carmody said nothing. Eight years of breaking granite boulders with a sledgehammer – and she thought he'd need a jack. He caught a corner of the buckboard in his right hand, balancing the wheel on the ground with his left.

'Oh, don't try to lift it, you'll break your back! There's a blacksmith just down the street, you can borrow a jack there.'

Carmody braced his feet, lifting with his right hand. The heavily-laden buckboard came slowly upright. He juggled the wheel into place, then stepped back and began threading the nut. He could feel the woman looking at him.

'You said you had a wrench, ma'am?'

She didn't answer, but he could hear rummaging under the seat. When she handed it to him their eyes met. He saw something in hers he didn't quite understand. Disapproval, maybe. Perhaps she thought he'd been showing off. No, it wasn't that. Maybe the mark of prison was still in his eyes.

He finished and stood up. 'That ought to hold,' he said.

'I'm much obliged,' she said sincerely.

There was a sudden clatter of hoofs and he heard the girl cry, 'Pinto, come back!' He turned and saw half a dozen riders coming down the street at a canter. The pup was racing toward them, yipping at the ponies' heels, oblivious to the shouts and curses of the riders as they fought their spooking mounts.

One of the riders pulled up short in front of them, his bronc wheeling in frenzy as the ball of black and white fur yipped at his fetlocks. 'Lady, git that gawdamn dawg of yours out'n the way afore I shoot the sonofabitch!'

Carmody saw the woman's face redden. 'Just control your horse, *and* your language, *Mister* Anson and ride on by. The pup won't follow. Penelope, stand back!'

At the mention of his name the rider jerked his eyes from the pup to glance at her. 'Oh, so it's you, Mrs Merriweather. . . .'

Merriweather! The name sent a tremor through Jeff Carmody and he jerked his head instinctively to look at her, his pulse quickening. Merriweather had had a wife, he'd heard. But she'd been back East at the time of the trial. Gone

7

back to Missouri so that her mother could look after her while she had her baby. He found himself looking at Penelope. Eight years ago. Yes, it was just possible. Good God!

The shock of hearing the name had driven everything else from his consciousness. It wasn't until he heard Penelope scream and the shot that followed that he jerked himself back to the present.

The pup rolled over in the dust under the impact of the heavy slug, kicked convulsively and lay still.

'. . . maybe that'll learn you to keep all your livestock out'n other folks way. An' if any more of your cows come driftin' onto my range after this they'll get the same medicine.'

Penelope was bent over the pitiful remains, stroking the still-warm fur while her mother stood ashen-faced, staring up at Anson.

Carmody broke out of his trance and stepped up beside the man's stirrup as Anson re-holstered his pistol. 'Get down,' Carmody said quietly.

Anson jerked his head to look at him. 'What did you say, mister?' he rasped in hoarse anger.

'You heard me,' Carmody said without raising his voice. 'I said get down.'

'Who the hell are you?'

'Never mind who I am – just do as I say.'

The man's hand whipped at the Colt. Carmody threw his arms in the air and yelled, 'Hold it! I haven't got a gun!'

Anson paused, then let the Colt slip back. 'Then maybe you'd better get one – or else don't go around shootin' off your mouth.'

Carmody was standing close to the man's stirrup, and now he slipped his hand under the latigo and closed his fist around it. It was like a shoestring in his grasp.

'You gonna get down?'

Anson glanced at Carmody, weighing him up. He was a big man himself, but he could see this angry youngster wasn't exactly puny. The advantage lay in the gun. If the stranger wanted to pick a fight with an armed man, then that was his own lookout.

'Why don't you try and make me?' he rasped.

There was a split-second of dead silence in which everybody froze, waiting.

Anson saw Carmody move and started his draw, but his target disappeared with the loud pop of the latigo breaking as Carmody heaved upwards, tearing saddle and rider from the horse's back. The other five sat in slack-jawed astonishment for just an instant before clawing for their guns, but Carmody knew what was coming and didn't wait. He jerked the bridle of Anson's mount and slapped the animal hard on the belly with the flat of his hand, sent him spinning into the five mounted men with resultant chaos. Anson landed on the flat of his shoulderblades, taking the weight of the saddle in his groin. He rolled, gasping painfully for breath, trying groggily to bring his gun to bear. Carmody flung himself on Anson, clamping one hand on the man's gun, shoving the other under his chin and forcing his head back till Anson's eyeballs showed white. The gun hand went limp and Carmody flipped the Colt, covering the others from a crouch.

'Hold it!' Carmody shouted in warning.

All movement ceased abruptly. The five mounted men glared down at him, some with half-drawn guns, still undecided.

'Holster and shuck 'em, boys,' Carmody said quietly.

Nobody moved.

The hammer clicked twice to full cock, unmistakably clear in the silence. 'I don't mean pretty soon – I mean *now!*'

In slow motion the guns slid away, angry fingers fumbled with gunbelts followed by the thud of gun harness in the dust. Carmody straightened, relaxed, and glanced at Anson stumbling to his feet.

'Saddle up, mister. It's hot standing here.'

Anson picked up saddle and blanket, dumping them on his mount. 'It's gonna be a damn sight hotter when I catch up with you, feller,' he gritted, looping the busted latigo without taking his eyes off Carmody.

'I'm scared stiff,' Carmody said.

Anson pulled himself painfully into the saddle and leaned heavily on the pommel. 'You ain't seen the last of me, fella.'

The man jerked his head to his riders to follow and they cantered off, riding stiff-backed and angry. Carmody followed them with his eyes till they were hidden in their own dust, then he turned around. Penelope was still holding the dog tightly to her.

'He's *dead*, Mommy,' she sobbed.

Mrs Merriweather leaned over and hugged the little girl to her, swallowing hard. She glanced up at Carmody. 'I-I don't know how to thank you,' she said with difficulty.

Carmody squatted in front of Penelope and ruffled the dead pup's ear. 'He ain't bad dead, little lady,' he said. 'He's just kind of busted up a little. Tell you what, why don't you let me have him for a day or two? Maybe I can fix him up.'

'Fix – fix him up!' Penelope's eyes widened with hope. 'Could you really, mister?'

Carmody saw the woman shaking her head at him, trying to save her daughter the torment of hoping for something that could never be. He gave her a solemn wink over Penelope's head and said, 'Well, I can't fix him myself. But I've got a doctor friend who's awful good with dogs. I'll take Pinto over there. He might not look exactly the same when you get him back, understand. Doc might have to put him back together a little different, shift the spots around some to get the pieces to fit. But it might take a little time.'

'Oh, I'll wait!' she said, holding the broken carcass out to him.

Carmody took it and turned to the buckboard. There was a gunnysack there and he took it out. As he turned around again he noticed people were beginning to come out of a few buildings along the boardwalk and stand staring in their direction now that the danger seemed past. He folded the gunnysack and laid the pup carefully on it. 'Reckon he ought to be comfortable like that till I get him to the doc,' he said convincingly.

While Penelope bent over the pup in wondering admiration, Carmody turned to her mother. 'Who's your friend?' he asked.

'Booth Anson? He owns the big spread next to our little place. Anson's Anvil. He's a troublemaker.'

'He didn't strike me as bein' real neighbourly.'

'Always pushing little people around. He's tried to buy me out, and when I wouldn't sell he started trying to make things so uncomfortable that I'd leave. But I guess I'm just stubborn. My husband got killed eight years ago. . . .

I know, Carmody thought. God, how well I know!

'. . . and since then it seems there's been nothing but trouble.' Then she smiled. 'Thanks, again, for all the help. Will we see you again?'

Carmody found himself smiling for the first time in eight long years. 'I reckon.'

'Anybody can tell you where we live,' she said, starting for the buckboard. Carmody gave her a hand up and lifted Penelope up beside her.

'What's your name, mister?' Penelope piped.

Carmody hesitated. 'Why – Jeff. Jeff Connolly.'

'Goodbye, Jeff,' she said solemnly.

Carmody stuffed Anson's gun inside his waistband and gathered the others, slinging the belts over his shoulder. Then he stepped up onto the boardwalk. Blank faces and curious stares followed him as he passed. Outside the barbershop one man ventured to ask, 'What was all the ruckus about, stranger?'

'What ruckus?' Carmody said, eyeing him.

11

The man edged back toward the door uneasily, sorry he'd opened his mouth. 'Why – nothin', I guess.'

'Where's the sheriff's office?'

The man pointed. 'Down there. Next to the post office. Mose ain't there, though. He rode to Canadian this morning early.'

'Mose?'

'Mose Dalmas. The sheriff.'

Carmody remembered now. He'd forgotten the name. So it was the same man that had been here eight years ago. If anybody would recognize him it would be Dalmas.

Carmody nodded and walked on. Outside the sheriff's office he stopped. There was a sign on the door: BE BACK TOMORROW. LEAVE ALL MESSAGES AT POST OFFICE.

The 'post office' turned out to be in a general store. A bald-headed oldster sitting behind the counter peered at him over steel spectacles. 'Where'd you get all them guns?' he said in amazement.

'Booth Anson's crowd,' Carmody said. 'If I leave them here will you give them to the sheriff when he comes back?'

The postmaster-storekeeper pulled a wooden soap box from under the counter. 'Dump 'em in there. I'll be right happy to see Mose gets 'em when he comes back.'

They buried the pup in a corner of the back yard, and when they had finished and put the spade away Carmody said, 'Any idea of where I can find another pup? I promised Penelope one.'

The old man scratched his bald head reflectively. 'That's a tall order, mister. Wait a minute though – seems I heard my wife talkin' about dogs last week. Hold on while I go ask her.' He went inside and opened a door that led to living quarters upstairs. 'Emmy!' he shouted. A woman's voice answered and he said, 'Wasn't you sayin' somethin' last week about somebody havin' a litter of pups they wanted to get rid of?' The woman said something Carmody couldn't hear and the man nodded and closed the door. When he came back he said, 'There's a rancher named Henstridge lives down on the Canadian river. They was up for supplies last week and his missus told my woman they had a litter of pups they was gonna have to get rid of. It's a long way, and they might have drowned 'em by now, but if you really want one and don't mind a long ride. . . .

'How far is it?'

' 'Bout ten mile. Take the stage trail to Canadian and branch off at the first creek you come to and follow the wagon track due south. You can't miss it.' Then he said, 'You a friend of Mrs Merriweather?'

'You might say I was.'

The man nodded. 'Thought I'd seen you around somewhere.'

Carmody asked, 'You seem to sell pretty near everything – you don't happen to carry Colt handguns, do you?'

The storekeeper turned back inside. 'Let's take a look. I think I got one or two somewheres about. One's second-hand, but it's in good shape.'

Carmody waited while he rummaged among various boxes on the shelves. 'Here they are,' he said, laying them on the counter. 'The new one comes kind of high. Thirteen-fifty. But I took the other one on trade and I can let you have it for five dollars. It's in good shape.'

Carmody inspected the new one first. It was a Remington .38. A good gun, but he was prejudiced against the calibre. He laid it aside and picked up the other, a Colt's frontier model .45. It had had good care, and the action was smooth. He bought it, plus a harness and box of cartridges. Then he inquired about a horse.

'There's a livery stable just down the street,' he was told.

'Thanks,' Carmody said.

At the door he remembered something and turned back. 'I see you carry a pretty good line of spurs.'

13

'Sure. I can fix you up with about any size you want.'

Carmody shook his head. 'I got mine down the street in my warbag. I just want some information.' He opened the flap of his shirt pocket and pulled out an object and dropped it on the counter. 'Ever sell anything like that?'

Gabe Ranson picked up the thing Carmody had dropped and adjusted his glasses. It was a spur rowel, three-quarter inch, eight pointed, with silver inlay radiating from the hole in the centre out along each spoke. 'Might have done,' he mused, turning it over. 'I've handled a lot in my day. Why, you tryin' to match a pair of rowels?'

Carmody reached for the rowel and put it back in his pocket, shaking his head. 'I just thought you might remember selling a pair with rowels like that. I'm looking for the man who lost this one.'

CHAPTER 2

It was nearly sundown when Jeff Carmody re-crossed the stage trail near the edge of the caprock high above the valley of the Canadian. Across the pommel in front of him lay a six-week-old pup.

The high plateau of the northern Panhandle lay before him, rolling a little, then gradually flattening until it stretched like a tabletop into the blue haze of evening dusk. Off to his left, toward the west, he caught the reflected light of the setting sun as it struck fire from the top of the water tank beside the depot at Sand Valley. The heat of the day had begun to fade, and already he caught the first breath of coolness of the approaching night. Shadow of horse and rider stretched long on the parched grassland, and inside his shirt the pup had fallen asleep, one paw and a black button nose visible between shirt buttons.

He was riding by starlight two hours later when he came down the gentle slope of the shallow valley set in the plateau and saw the yellow square of lamplight among the cottonwoods. He had taken longer than he expected. There had been a detour – a stretch of barbed wire that seemed endless as he rode to get around it. Barbed wire, he thought with regret, had spread fast in the past eight years. He had been surprised to see how much there was on the train ride from Huntsville. Too much. He didn't like it. And he liked this

15

particular stretch less when he came to the corner where it veered suddenly off to the north and had read the sign. ANVIL RANCH. BOOTH ANSON, PROP. KEEP OUT!

As he splashed across the creek and rode through the cottonwoods he saw the Merriweather woman framed in the lamplight in the doorway, brought there by the sound of his approach. Then, closer, another figure raised itself. A man, with a rifle in his hand.

'Hold it right there, mister!' a voice called.

Carmody reined in.

'It's all right, fella – I come peaceable,' he said quietly. At the sound of his voice the woman stepped out of the house. 'Is that you, Mister Connelly?' she said.

'That's right,' Carmody said. 'I brought something for your little girl.'

She caught her breath. 'Not – not the pup!'

Carmody handed the squirming bundle down to her. She caught it and turned to the man with the rifle and said quickly, 'Caleb, you can put your gun down. This man's a friend. Mr Connelly, this is the foreman and entire crew of the Merriweather ranch, Caleb Stockbridge.'

Caleb, Carmody saw as he leaned down to shake hands, was in his middle sixties or thereabouts. 'Howdy, Connelly,' the man said.

'Jeff'll do, Caleb,' Carmody said, surprised at how easily he was growing into his alias.

Caleb motioned to him, saying, 'Water trough's over this way – Carmody.'

Jeff felt himself tighten all over. 'The name's Connolly, Caleb,' he said, trying to make it sound casual.

'Not unless you changed it in the last eight years, it ain't,' Caleb answered quietly.

For a moment their eyes met and held in the starlight. 'Does she know?' Carmody said.

'I don't reckon she'd've given you such a howdy-do if she

did. She ain't never got over it.'

'I'm sorry to hear that,' Carmody said with considerable feeling. 'But I didn't kill him, Caleb. Maybe you won't believe that, after the trial I had and all, but it's the truth.'

A flurry of excitement prevented Caleb's reply as Penelope burst out of the house wearing a nightgown, carrying the pup who was barking his head off with enthusiasm at the reception he'd had. 'Jeff!' Penelope shrieked with delight. 'Jeff, he's almost like *new*.'

Carmody tried to smile but realized he was making a bad job of it after what Caleb had just said. 'I think Doc did a pretty good job. I'll tell him you're pretty well satisfied.'

'Penelope, you're supposed to be in bed now,' her mother called.

The girl put the pup on the ground and ran toward the house with it following at her heels. 'G'night, Jeff!' she called.

'You weren't thinking of leaving tonight?' Penelope's mother said. 'Why can't you stay over?'

'Thanks, Mrs Merriweather, but I've got to get back to. . . .'

He felt Caleb's elbow dig him in the ribs. 'He don't neither, Anne,' the old man said. 'He's just tryin' to be perlite. Why, just before you come out he was tellin' me how tuckered he was after ridin' all day. Besides,' he added, turning to Carmody. 'I was kind of lookin' forward to finishin' that chat we'd started.'

'You'll stay then, Mister Connolly?' Anne said.

Carmody nodded. 'Much obliged, ma'am.'

'I'm glad,' she said with a smile. 'You look tired. Caleb, show him where to put his horse then you two wash up and come on in. I'll go put supper on the table.'

Caleb led the way to the pole corral, and when Carmody's mount had been watered and turned inside the two of them washed. Caleb indicated that Carmody, as guest, should wash first, then said, 'I know you didn't kill Clint Merriweather, son.'

Carmody paused in the act of rolling up his sleeves and

17

glanced at the leathered old face peering earnestly at him in the starlight. 'Do you really mean that?' he asked bluntly.

Caleb nodded.

'Does she think I killed him?'

The old man heaved a sigh and stood up, nodding. 'If she thought you was who you are. . . . I told her all along that it didn't make sense. Why would a complete stranger like yourself want to kill a man you ain't never seen before?'

'The jury believed it,' Carmody said with a tinge of bitterness.

Caleb snorted. 'Jury, hell!' he said in disgust. 'That bunch of hammerheads was picked just because they'd believe what somebody wanted 'em to believe.'

'I spent eight years in Huntsville,' Carmody said quietly. 'Eight years breaking up granite boulders in a sun so hot it makes Hell look cool by comparison – or in the wintertime shivering in a cell when the only thing to keep you warm was the memory of the exercise you'd had breaking those boulders. Eight years, Caleb. Eight years paying for a killing somebody else did.' He lowered his voice to a hoarse whisper. 'Who was it, Caleb?'

Caleb shook his head sadly. 'I don't know, son. If I did I'd have gone after him long ago, old as I am, for killin' Clint.'

The house was only a few yards away and a shadow fell across them in the pale lamplight as Anne came to the door. 'Caleb! If you keep Mister Connelly out there talking all night his supper'll be cold.'

Before they got to the door Carmody asked, 'How long has Booth Anson been in these parts?'

'Since away back. But if you're thinkin' he might've done it, don't. Not that I'd put it past him – it's just the kind of thing he'd enjoy doin'. Especially since he's been tryin' to get hold of this place for a long time. Killin' Clint might've looked like one way to get it.'

'Then what makes you so sure he didn't?'

18

'He was down in Canadian the night it happened. Twenty miles away.'

'He might have said he was down in Canadian – or got somebody else to say it. Money talks.'

Caleb sighed. 'That's just the hell of it, Jeff. . . .'

Carmody caught his elbow. 'You'd better learn to call me Jeff,' he said, glancing toward the door. 'If she finds out. . . .'

'I'd better watch that, all right. Good thing you picked a name that sounded like the other. It might cover a slip of the tongue sometime.'

'You were saying something about Anson,' Carmody said as he moved away again.

'Oh, yeah . . . well, he was down in Canadian that night. I saw him. I was there.'

After supper that night Carmody and Caleb went outside and sat on a bench in the starlight.

'Pretty nice spot,' Carmody commented. 'Nice sheltered valley, good running water. Spring?'

Caleb nodded, puffing his pipe. 'Good spring, too. Rises 'bout two miles up the valley. I've never seen it run dry, even in the longest drought.'

'This creek runs on east across Anson's place, I guess?'

'Nope, that's the funny thing. There's a piece of bogland down the creek a few miles. The creek spreads out over a bed of quicksand and marsh grass and just plumb disappears. Goes underground. Don't come out again till clear down on the Canadian ten miles below. That's one reason Anson's so hot about tryin' to get hold of this place. That creek sinks out of sight just about a hundred yards short of his fence.'

'He short of water?'

'He's got a few lakes. You know what that's like. Go bone dry just when you need 'em most.'

'You said that was one reason,' Carmody said. 'He's got others?'

19

'Yep. He owns 'bout fifteen sections to the east of here, and pretty near the same size range to the west of us. We're right smack dab in the middle, cuttin' his range right in two.'

'How'd that happen?'

'Well, it goes back a long way. Anson bought up a place 'way east of here years back to begin with. Then he started spreadin' out. Bought some. Stole some. Leastwise, he pushed people until they moved and sold it for next to nothin'.'

Carmody was silent for a long time, moody with thought. Finally he said, 'That makes it look all the more like Anson's the man I'm looking for – the man who killed Clint Merriweather.'

'Yeah,' Caleb sighed, 'I tried to figure it that way, too. But I seen him in Canadian with my own eyes just before the time Clint was bein' bushwhacked.'

'He could have paid somebody to do it for him.'

'I've often wondered about that, too,' Caleb said reflectively. 'Only there wasn't a single man in this part of the Panhandle that wasn't a good friend to Clint Merriweather. An' damn few who didn't hate Booth Anson's guts. If he hired it done, it had to be a stranger.'

Carmody looked at him. 'What makes you so sure it wasn't me that did it, then?'

The old man shrugged. 'I can't explain it. But in sixty-five winters I've learned a little about human nature. You just ain't the kind, that's all.'

Carmody fell silent, thinking. He thought of the spur rowel and dug it out of his pocket. 'Ever see this before?' he said, handing it to Caleb. The old man studied it for a long time, turning it over and over, before handing it back. 'No. Can't say I have. Where'd you get it?'

'Found it laying on the trail beside Clint's body the night he got shot.'

'It wasn't Clint's, I can vouch for that.'

Carmody nodded. 'That was the first thing I checked.'

'Then you figure it belonged to the man who shot him?'

'I'm dead certain.'

'You showed it to Mose Dalmas when he arrested you, didn't you?'

'Yep. All he said was, "Carmody, there's maybe sixty-thousand men in the state of Texas wears spurs. Any one of them could've lost that rowel."'

Caleb puffed awhile in silence. 'The hell of it is, son, he's dead right,' he said reluctantly. 'For that matter, he might've thought you'd planted it there yourself to throw him off.'

'Yeah – he mentioned that, too.'

The old man shook his head and stood up. 'Clint was a mighty fine man, son. I hope you find whoever did it. But it looks like you've got a cold trail to follow.'

Carmody stood up slowly. 'But I'll find him, Caleb,' he said quietly. 'If it takes me the rest of my life and ten thousand miles of riding, I'll find him.'

Carmody walked off, making his way past the corrals and toward the cottonwoods beside the creek. He found a deep pool and sat down beside it, resting his back against a tall cottonwood. The night was still warm here in the little valley; it would be cooler up on the plateau above, but down here it was sheltered. A good spot to winter stock in, he thought. The creek probably never froze solid, so there'd be plenty of water. And the slope of the hills would cut off the worst of the northwesters.

CHAPTER 3

The following morning, Carmody had finished breakfast and was rolling a cigarette to go with his second cup of coffee when he asked, 'Penelope around this morning?'

Anne smiled. 'She's down along the creek.'

Carmody drank his coffee and stood up. 'I'll ride by and say goodbye to her on my way out.'

'You're leaving us?' Anne said, her disappointment showing plainly in her voice.

Carmody looked at her. 'I didn't aim to become a star boarder just on the strength of a mongrel pup.'

'I didn't mean it that way,' she said quickly. 'I just thought – well, you don't seem to be tied down. If you're looking for a job. . . .'

The offer came as a surprise. He had no idea of how big a spread she had but it seemed reasonable that it would be a small one since Caleb was her only hand. It hadn't occurred to him that she might need help.

Anne misinterpreted his hesitation. 'I suppose you're like all the rest – you hate the idea of working for a woman.' There was no bitterness in the remark, but he thought he detected a note of despair.

'No, ma'am,' he said firmly. 'Your money's as good a pay as anybody's. I didn't know you needed a hand, that's all.'

'Need a hand? I need half a dozen. When Clint was alive we

22

had the bunkhouse full and two extra bunks in the barn. But since he died – well, like I said . . . most men seem to hate the idea of working for a woman. It does something to their pride. I've had a few, off and on, but they soon drift. Old Caleb's stuck with me through it all, but the two of us can't manage alone. I've had to cut down on the herd until we can just barely pay our way at the bank. And between that and Booth Anson. . . .' She broke off and turned away.

Carmody was lost in thought. A job here would have its advantages. Caleb already knew who he was and what he was after. That could be a big help. Besides, Anne Merriweather was already having trouble with Anson. A job here would provide Carmody with a convenient excuse to keep an eye on Anson – for some reason he still felt certain that Anson was behind the killing of Clint.

There were two disadvantages, and Carmody marked them well in his mind before reaching a decision. If he took a job here he would be taking on somebody else's troubles and it might mean, if his hunch about Anson was wrong, that his own cause would suffer. But the second disadvantage bothered him most. Living this close to Anne Merriweather increased the danger that she would find out his true identity. A slip of the tongue, a chance visit by somebody who might recognize him, and the secret would be out. For some reason he didn't want her to know who he was until he had cleared his name.

'You've got a hand,' he said suddenly.

She turned away from the window. 'I don't want you to take the job just because you feel sorry for me,' she said evenly. 'But you've got a right to know, if you're going to work here. I have got troubles. You've met Booth Anson, so you know what you'd be up against. He's trying to get me off this land.'

'Caleb told me.'

'And you still want the job?'

'I don't scare easy, Mrs Merriweather.'

'You'd better learn to call me Anne, Jeff. Mrs Merriweather

makes me feel my widowhood too much.' Then, as if this sounded too sombre, she added with a smile, 'And everybody thinks of a widow as being at least fifty. Female vanity, I guess. No woman likes the thought of growing old.'

That was something she wouldn't have to worry about for a long time, Carmody thought. But the ground was too personal to tread just now and he avoided it. Changing the subject he said, 'You've got horses, I suppose? I ought to take that livery mount back to town.'

'Caleb will help you pick your string.' Then she smiled bemusedly. 'You're a funny man, Jeff. You ask about horses, but you didn't bother to ask about your pay.'

Carmody shrugged. 'Thirty and found. That's usual, isn't it?'

'Sixty.'

He pursed his lips. 'You could hire two men for that.'

'Don't worry,' she said with a firm smile. 'You'll do two men's work on this range.'

Carmody looked at her in new appraisal. There had been no sarcasm in the remark. Just a plain statement of fact. He felt a warm admiration for this woman who refused to knuckle under to Booth Anson, despite the odds.

She put out her hand. 'Is it a deal, then?'

He took her hand and found the grip was surprisingly strong for one so feminine. 'It's a deal,' he said.

When he stepped out of the house he noticed a commotion down by the corral and saw it was Caleb crowding a bunch of saddle stock inside the bars. He crossed the yard and leaned against the corral to peer inside while Caleb closed the gate and got down to light his pipe.

'Not a bad looking bunch,' Carmody commented.

'Clint always kept a pretty good saddle stock,' Caleb said, puffing at his pipe. 'Held onto a good stud and a few good brood mares and culled out the rest.' He stabbed his pipestem at the corral. 'Most of them was colts when Clint got killed.

'Fraid they ain't been exactly gentled – I'm a little too old for that kind of work and we ain't been able to keep a good wrangler on the place. But if you ain't afraid to take the rough edges off a few of 'em you ought to make up a pretty good string with the best of these.'

Two hours later Carmody got down stiff-legged from a sweating bronc, jerked off the saddle and dumped it over a corral rail. 'I reckon that'll do, Caleb. I'll keep those last five up here and turn the rest out.' He wiped the sweat from his face. 'I sure got rusty in eight years.'

Caleb dug an elbow into his ribs and said quietly, 'Here comes Anne. She hears you talkin' like that she might start wonderin' where you been them eight years.'

Carmody glanced up as Anne approached. He'd never seen a woman in men's garb before and it jolted him a little. Especially since the voluminous calico dresses in which he had previously seen her had only hinted at what he saw now.

Anne noticed his look and smiled her amusement. 'You didn't expect me to work in skirts, did you, Jeff?'

Carmody stirred out of his trance. 'I hadn't thought about it,' he said.

She turned to Caleb. 'Anson said yesterday that my cows were still wandering through his fence. I know where they're getting through, but it's his fence, not ours. If he wants to keep them out it's up to him, not us. But I think I'll ride down and have a look anyway. Jeff has to take that livery mount back to town, so he can ride that far with me.'

Anne lifted a rope from a corral post and built a loop with an expert flip of the wrist, walking towards the horses still standing in the corral. Carmody started forward, intending to catch her mount for her but Caleb's hand on his arm restrained him. 'She ain't helpless, son,' the old man chuckled.

Carmody leaned slowly back into his former position against the post, his cigarette dangled forgotten from his lips as he watched Anne. Two or three of her own mounts had been in the corral when Caleb had run the others in, and it was one of these she was after now. Eleven horses altogether. Carmody had seen good ropers unashamedly take more than one loop to pick out a mount in a bunch like this; but then he imagined that her own private horses would be more gentled and would probably stand for her when the others moved away.

Anne crossed the corral slowly, the loop dragging behind her, half-hidden by her body from the now-milling animals. Two of the wilder ones now spooked and crowded the others and all eleven were off, running wall-eyed in a close-packed mass half-hidden in the cloud of rising dust. He saw the loop sail through the air and settle, and when the dust cleared a little he saw she had snared a blaze-faced bay from the middle of the bunch and was bracing herself as she worked him pitching and fighting toward the snubbing post. Her movements were cool and sure, she let the struggling mount do most of the work, and when his head came down she took slack and half-hitched him quickly to the post and turned to pick her saddle from the corral rail.

Carmody turned to Caleb with a questioning glance. 'She ain't going to *ride* that one?' he said quietly.

'Watch,' was all Caleb said.

Anne soft-talked the quivering mount as she blanketed and saddled him and he quietened a little. But Carmody knew instinctively from the way the bay watched her that soft-talk alone would not be enough. She favoured a hackamore, he noticed, and that moved him to genuine admiration, both for her ability and her savvy. The bay was by no means gentled, but it stood quietly when she slipped off the rope and coiled it, restraining him only on the hackamore rein.

Anne mounted quickly, and Carmody was glad to see her distract the bay by earing him down as she swung up. The bay was in motion sideways but she found her seat without effort and seemed to take genuine satisfaction in the fact he still showed fight. When he felt her weight the bay stopped sidling and took off straight up, shaking the ground as he hit hard on his forefeet and straightening his back with a kick of his hind legs that slapped the saddle hard along his backbone, showing daylight between skirt and blanket. But Anne was still there, glued to the saddle through all the crazy angles and tickling his ribs with a fluid fore and aft motion as she raked him in the rhythm of his jumps. The bay knew he was saddled for the day and settled for a final attempt to gallop around the corral, but she hackamored him to a halt and let him get his wind while she turned to Carmody.

'All set, Jeff,' she said. There was nothing in her voice to show that she considered the feat unusual, even for a woman. She was merely a working rancher who had saddled a frisky horse and was now waiting for one of her hands to saddle his own mount and join her.

Carmody only nodded and picked up his saddle. The last of the string he had just topped was tied outside the corral alongside the livery mount. He dumped the saddle in place and as he tightened the cinch he glanced back at Anne now talking quietly to Caleb and he felt glad that he had already taken the edge off the horse he was now saddling. Any show of fight now, no matter how well he rode, would make him look clumsy in comparison with what he had just seen. He mounted up and took the rented horse in tow, reining in beside Anne as she came out of the corral while Caleb held the gate.

They rode in silence for awhile, across the creek through the cottonwoods and up the long slope that led out of the little valley. Finally Carmody's curiosity got the better of him. He turned to her and said off-handedly, 'Where'd you learn to ride like that?'

She mistook his question for criticism, glancing mechanically down at her saddle, stirrups, hackamore. Finding no fault with the way she rode she looked up at him, puzzled, and asked, 'Like what?'

'I mean, like you did back there. Who taught you to ride like that?'

'My father. Why, do you find it strange that a woman should be able to ride?' The question was guileless.

Carmody said wryly, 'No, not exactly. I've seen a few women ride.' He shoved back his hat and added, 'Side-saddle. On a gentle horse.'

She smiled, and there was a touch of bitterness in the smile. 'I was an only child. My father wanted a son. He never had one. We had a big horse ranch up in Wyoming Territory. He made his living breaking and selling stock to the cavalry. I guess he'd counted on a son being a big help to him. When my mother died and he lost all chance of having a son I guess he decided I'd have to make up for what I'd done to his life. I was running wild mustangs when I was only twelve. By the time I was fourteen I was breaking them. I just grew up that way and never thought there was anything strange in it. I seldom saw another woman and it wasn't until I married Clint and came here that I found I was a little different. But it didn't bother me much, except' – she turned to smile at him – 'except that I learned to wear skirts in town to keep "decent" women from staring at me like I was a fallen woman.'

Carmody rode on for a while in thoughtful silence. Then he said, 'Did your husband let you ride, rough ones, I mean?'

She laughed. 'Good heavens, no! Clint nearly had a fit when he first met me at a horse camp up in Wyoming. And it took him a long time to even get used to the idea of me wearing men's clothes around the ranch after we were married. He bought me the first dress I ever owned. And I guess he thought that when Penelope came along it would change things for good – turn me into a real housewife and mother instead of a half-wild horsewoman.' Her laughter faded. 'But he never lived to see Penelope.'

She stopped talking and Carmody felt sorry the conversation

had strayed as it had. But something she had said somewhere along the line disturbed him vaguely, though he couldn't exactly put his finger on it. Then suddenly he realized what it was. During the trial he'd heard that Anne Merriweather had been sent East to her mother to have her baby. But she'd just said she had no mother. He tried a gentle question.

'Must've been pretty hard on you, losing your husband. Didn't he have any folks or anything around here you could go to?'

She shook her head. He had an old aunt back East. It was Caleb's sister, really. But he called her his aunt, even though he'd only seen her once when she came out to visit Caleb years back. They both insisted that I go back to stay with her and have Penelope there. They said a ranch with no woman around wasn't a fit place for me to have a baby.' Her tone saddened again. 'I was back there when Clint got killed. I didn't even get to the funeral, of course. So far away. Even the trial of the man who killed him was over when I got back.' Her voice grew distant and she seemed not to be talking to him but to herself. 'I don't know why, but I wanted to see that man. Maybe – maybe I wanted to tell him how much I hated him for what he'd done to me. Clint and I had only been married eighteen months. That's a short time, Jeff – a short time to be happy in. And those eighteen months were the only happy months I'd ever known.'

She fell quiet for a minute and Carmody did not intrude on her thoughts. Then suddenly she said in a quiet voice, 'They didn't hang the man who killed Clint. The judge said he wanted to be lenient because he wasn't twenty-one. And there was some legal question that I didn't understand – something about him just trying to rob Clint and the killing being more or less accidental. I don't remember how long he was sent to prison for. Ten years, I think. . . .'

With time off for good behaviour makes it eight, Carmody was thinking.

'. . . so he should be out soon. I've been meaning to write to the warden at Huntsville and ask to be told when he's set free. Maybe I'll do that and. . . .' She didn't finish. The rhythmic beat of their horses' hoofs sounded loud in the silence; but not loud enough to cover the hatred in her voice.

Carmody said nothing.

CHAPTER 4

When they came within sight of Anson's fence Anne reined in and pointed, saying, 'There's where the trouble is; where that gully cuts down the side of the slope into my place. The gully's too steep to plant fence posts, so Anson just strung the wire across and weighted it down with rocks. It works all right to keep his cows in, because they graze right up to the edge of the gully and then turn back to find more grass. But my cows start in to graze down here where the gully widens out and they just wander uphill where it narrows like a funnel and leads them under the fence and out onto Anson's land. There's plenty of clearance under the fence because the rocks don't weight it clear to the ground. You'll see better when we get down a little closer.'

They had just started to ride on when the whipsnap of a rifle shot reached them. Another followed after a short interval. Then two more.

'Sounded like down there in that gully someplace,' Carmody said. Remembering Anson's threat to shoot Anne's straying cattle, both clapped spurs to their horses simultaneously. They were still a quarter of a mile from the gully when they saw a thin column of dust rising from the bottom of it, but whatever was raising the dust was still hidden by the steep banks. Then Carmody gave a shout and pointed. Well inside Anson's fence where the gully headed on high ground a rider appeared. He was heading away from them, moving fast, sliding a rifle back into its boot as he rode. Four steers lay dead on the gully floor, the blood glistening as it seeped from the bulletholes in their foreheads.

Carmody raised his head and peered up the length of he gully into Anson's territory. 'Recognize that fella?' he asked quietly.

Anne nodded, biting her lip to keep back angry tears. 'Neaf Hacker. He was with that bunch you met in town yesterday when they shot Pinto.'

Something down below drew Carmody's attention. He examined the ground below the fence carefully for a minute, then went back to his horse and remounted and joined Anne.

'I wondered how that fella raised so much dust,' he said as he came up beside her.

'What did you find?'

Carmody pointed into the gully. 'See those marks down there? Your steers were on their own ground when they were shot. Your friend Hacker dragged them up where they are now to make it look like they'd strayed.' Then he added grimly, 'Not that it makes a hell of a lot of difference. He had no right to shoot 'em either side of the fence. If Anson wants your cattle kept out, let him string his wire lower down.'

'Well,' Carmody sighed, 'neither cussin' nor cryin's gonna help get your steers back. How much are they worth on the market right now.'

She studied for a minute. 'They were yearlings just coming two – about fourteen dollars a head on the siding. Maybe sixteen in Kansas City.'

'Call it sixteen,' Carmody said. He slid his Colt from its holster, flipped open the loading gate and spun the cylinder to check the load. 'You catch that livery mount and take him back to your place. I can take him to town some other time. Right now I'm going to collect.'

She looked at him in alarm. 'Collect? Collect what?'

'Why – the money for them steers, that's what.' He screwed up his face with the agony of mental arithmetic, 'Let's see – sixteen a head, four steers.'

'Sixty-four dollars,' she snapped, 'and don't think I'm going to let you do a fool thing like riding up to Booth Anson's front door and ask him for it.'

He looked at her in amazement. 'You know of any other way to get it?'

'If he got you inside his territory he'd shoot you and have a dozen witnesses to say it was self-defence.'

Carmody raised an eyebrow. 'Supposin' I shot first?'

She shook her head violently. 'No, Jeff – I won't let you. It's not worth it.'

'Supposin' I go anyway?'

'Then you're fired,' she said firmly.

Carmody said nothing, staring across the fence into Anson's range.

Anne turned the bay around. 'Might as well catch up your livery horse and we'll ride into town together. Mose Dalmas ought to be back from Canadian by now. We'll tell him what happened – for all the good it'll do.'

'The sheriff?' Carmody said. 'Why'd you say it like that – is he scared of Anson or something?'

She nodded. 'At least I think so from the way Anson's crowd has the run of the town when they're there. Mose just shrugs off their shenanigans as high spirits; but I think he's afraid Anson is too much for him to handle. Anyway, we'll soon find out. This is the first time anything this serious has come up. It might make a difference.'

Carmody was turning the thing over in his mind as they rode back to where the livery mount cropped at the parched grass. A visit to the sheriff, in Anne's company, was something he wanted to avoid. Dalmas would be sure to remember him from eight years back. Anne's bitter hatred of the man she thought had killed her husband would blind her to any reasoning Carmody might produce.

He reached out and caught the lead rope to take the rented buckskin in tow and the idea dawned. He hesitated, glancing back in the direction of the gully. 'Seems a shame to waste all that good beef,' he mused aloud.

He could see Anne turn to follow his gaze. 'Can't do much about it in this heat,' she said regretfully.

'Got any salt back at the house' Carmody said slyly.

'Y-e-ss!' she said. 'I could get Caleb to help me. We could load a couple of barrels of salt in the spring wagon and bring it out here and butcher on the spot. At least we could save some of the meat for winter.' She turned and eyed Carmody who was calmly puffing a cigarette and gazing at nothing in particular. 'You could go to the sheriff, couldn't you – tell him what happened? I'd go with you, but since I've got to go get Caleb and you're going in anyway. . . .'

Carmody straightened in the saddle and pulled his hat down. 'Sure, I don't mind,' he said. 'I'll come back soon as I can and give you a hand saltin' down that beef.' He was turning away when she called to him.

'Jeff!'

He turned around. 'Yeah?'

'You're not thinking of sneaking off to collar Booth Anson when my back's turned, are you?'

Carmody grinned. 'And get myself fired? No thankee, ma'am. I'll do it real legal-like, the way you want it. But I'm kind of hoping you're right about the sheriff bein' scared of Anson.'

'Why?' she asked, puzzled.

'Because then you'll have to let me ride up to Anson and get your sixty-four dollars back.' Still grinning at her, he raised his hand and touched his spurs to his mount, cantering off in the direction of town.

Anne sat watching him for a minute till he disappeared over a rise. Then her frown relaxed and gradually gave way to a smile. 'Cocky son-of-a-gun!' she said aloud. She turned and rode away slowly with a thoughtful expression. It was difficult to believe she had known this man less than twenty-four hours. Yet in that time she felt he had done something to her life; entered it with a kind of easy permanence as if he belonged there. Still, he hadn't really done anything to make her feel like that. Well – he had stood up to Booth Anson over the pup yesterday. But any man who might have happened along would have done the same. Then she shook her head quickly. No, not just any man. He hadn't even been wearing a gun there.

She'd had that feeling about him that morning when she offered him a job. She knew, like it was part of a plan, that he wouldn't refuse. Other men she'd hired in the past eight years had been different. Some of them had got big ideas – here was a young widow with a ranch. Others had just been plain worthless; either they were constantly trying to climb in through her bedroom window or else they went completely the other way and began to hate her when they realized they were actually working for a woman. But all of them had drifted on. Carmody wouldn't. She knew. Not that there was anything like that mixed up with her feelings for him. But there was something comfortable in having him around. Something solid.

It gave her a start to realize that the only other man who had ever come riding into her life so completely in focus was Clint Merriweather.

She shook her head quickly and put her mount into a lope as if to leave this disturbing thought far behind.

It was high noon when Carmody rode into Sand Valley and reined in at Buckley's livery. He dismounted and watered the horses. Then he lifted the tin cup from the pump and filled it, drinking the cool water in slow gulps.

Buck Buckley came out while he was drinking and leaned

against the doorframe. Carmody turned around.

'Hot, ain't it?' Buckley said.

'Hot enough,' Carmody answered. 'Brought your nag back in one piece. How much do I owe you?'

Buckley ran his eyes over the rented horse. 'Don't look like you damaged him much. Make it seventy-five cents – fifty for the horse and two-bits for the saddle.'

Carmody paid him and asked, 'Sheriff back yet?'

The other nodded. 'Seen him ride in early this morning.' Then he glanced at the horse Carmody was riding. 'M.W.' he said. 'That's the Merriweather brand. You ridin' for Anne?'

Carmody mounted up. 'That's right,' he said and rode off. He swung down in front of the sheriff's office and tied up.

Mose Dalmas looked up from his desk at the sound of Carmody's boot heels and Carmody saw the gimlet eyes search his face while the lawman's own face remained dead-pan. But there was recognition in the eyes.

'What can I do for you, mister?' Dalmas said.

'Did you get those guns I left at the post office yesterday?'

Dalmas frowned, giving Carmody a quick glance of reappraisal. 'Yeah, I got them. Mind tellin' me exactly what happened?'

Carmody ignored the question for one of his own. 'Did Anson pick them up?'

The sheriff nodded. 'Sent a man in early this morning.'

'What did he say happened?'

'Well – he said a crazy dog tried to hamstring Booth's horse and that when Booth shot the dog you jumped him from behind and jerked his gun away and disarmed the whole bunch.'

Carmody chuckled. 'You believe that?'

'Well – when Gabe Ranson brought them guns in here he said he'd heard that the Merriweather girl's dog had bothered Booth's horse. . . .'

'Dog?' Carmody said, interrupting. 'You sure he didn't say pup?'

Dalmas hedged. 'Well – maybe he did. Anyway, it don't make much difference. Point is you took a lot onto yourself interferin' with a man tryin' to protect his horse. Who are you, anyway? I seem to recollect seein' you before somewheres.'

Carmody hooked the rung of a chair with the toe of his boot, drew it toward him and sat down. 'Name's Connelly,' he said blandly. 'Jeff Connelly. And now that we're acquainted I'll put my cards on the table and you can make up your mind whether you're sheriff of this county or afraid of Booth Anson. You can't be both.'

Dalmas purpled with anger and half-rose. 'What's your game, mister?' he gritted.

'I got no game, sheriff. I just want to know whether you're on the side of the law or the man with the most guns. Booth Anson shot a little girl's six-week-old pup and I pulled him off his horse. The pup was only barking, and he wasn't big enough to bite a good-sized mouse. I'm pretty sure you know that already, but from the way you're talking I got a hunch you'd just as soon look the other way when Booth Anson does anything.'

Dalmas started to speak but Carmody silenced him with a gesture. 'You know it wasn't just the pup that bothered Anson. He's got his hackles up because Anne Merriweather's place splits his range in two and she won't sell out to him. So he's decided to be nasty. This morning,' he said slowly, 'he got real nasty. One of his riders shot four of Anne's steers. That's why I'm here.'

Dalmas sat back down, swallowing hard. Carmody could see that the seriousness of the situation had rocked him a little. This was not just a case of Booth Anson's crew getting drunk and roistering around town. Four steers had been shot. This was cattle country. The cattlemen's vote had put Dalmas in office. It could take him out.

'This time,' Carmody said pointedly, 'it's going to be hard for you to just look the other way.'

37

'I don't like your insinuation, Connelly,' Dalmas snapped. 'I've held office in this county for the past fifteen years with a clear record for honesty and impartiality. And I don't aim to let you come in here and make smart-alec remarks. If you got a case, let's hear it.'

Carmody grinned. 'That's better, sheriff. One of Anson's riders shot four of Anne's steers. All you got to do is get Anson to fork over an apology and sixty-four dollars compensation and we'll forget the whole thing.'

Dalmast picked up a pen from his desk and twirled it absently between his fingers. 'How do you fit into this? What business is it of yours?'

'I work for Anne Merriweather. She sent me in to you to straighten this thing out.'

The sheriff sat back, frowning. 'Well – you're making a mighty tall accusation, mister. I know Anne Merriweather and Booth don't get along too well, but before I go stirrin' anything up I got to have somethin' to go on. Just because somebody shot four of her steers ain't no sign Anson did it.'

'You've got something to go on. This ain't guesswork. We heard the shots, saw Neaf Hacker ride out of the gully and found the steers dead. What's more, he'd dragged them under the fence to make it look like they'd strayed onto Anvil range. Not that it would make any difference.'

Dalmas sat for a while without saying anything. He didn't look at Carmody. Finally he said, 'Well – maybe I'd better go investigate.'

Carmody could feel the insincerity behind the words and felt his own anger rising. He stood up. 'All right, sheriff. We'll ride out together.'

'I've found my way around this county for twenty years, Connelly. I think I can still manage without any help.'

Carmody stared at him for a full half minute without blinking, fighting down his anger. Then he heaved a big sigh and said patiently, 'When'll you let Anne know the results of this "investigation" of yours, sheriff?'

'Oh, sometime tomorrow, I reckon.'

Carmody nodded and turned slowly toward the door. Half-way there he paused and glanced back. 'Y'know something, Dalmas? There's only one thing lower than a man who'd shoot a little girl's pup – and that's the man who'd try to protect him.'

With deliberate slowness he turned and walked out of the door.

CHAPTER 5

Carmody stepped down off the boardwalk and stood for a long minute in gloomy contemplation, squinting his eyes as a gust of hot wind eddied the dust around him. The town lay quiet and empty under the leaden heat of post-noon. In front of the Sand Valley Cattleman's Rest a solitary pinto switched flies with head bowed resignedly. He remembered his own mount then and the creeping apprehension now broke over him in a sudden flood and he jerked his head in the direction of the willow scrub.

The horse was gone. There was a faint chance that the dun might have slipped the reins from the willow branch and wandered between the buildings. But even as he stepped down to have a look Carmody knew that was not the answer. With tension tingling the nerves along his backbone he came around the corner between the buildings. Then he stopped.

There were four of them. Waiting for him. The right hand of each man rested significantly on the butt of his gun. Carmody had a vague recollection of having seen their faces with Anson's bunch the previous day. The man nearest him spoke after an interval.

'Lookin' for somethin', Connelly?' The words, and the grin that accompanied them, were calculated, Carmody knew, to stir him to some foolish action.

'Well, I was looking for my horse,' he said with a casualness he did not feel. 'But it looks like I found four jackasses instead.'

One of the men behind the leader stiffened away from the wall with a sudden movement, jerking his gun and snarling something. The man who had spoken threw his arm out at waist-level, blocking the draw. 'Hold it, Hallstead!' he barked.

Carmody had bent his knees, crouching to draw, his hand ready. 'Let him go if he wants to,' he said quietly. There was a tense moment of silence in which the two glared at each other, but Carmody felt deep relief when the first man made Hallstead shove his gun away. Against Hallstead alone he would have had better than an even chance. But with three more waiting he would never have lived to tell about it and he knew it.

'Why'd you stop me, Creekmore?' Hallstead rasped.

Creekmore ignored him and turned back to Carmody. 'Was that your horse?' he said in mock surprise, raising his eyebrows. 'Well, now, that's a real laugh. We seen the brand and figgered it'd strayed from the Merriweather place – so we turned it loose and left it to find its own way home. Now ain't that a shame?'

'That's all right, Creekmore,' Carmody said tightly, 'I ain't proud – I'll ride your horse.'

The man straightened slowly. 'You're real tall, ain't you, fella?'

'Tall enough to reach the ground when I stand up – maybe you'd like to cut me down a little?'

While Creekmore stared at him Carmody heard the sound of a train whistle muffled by distance and heat. Hallstead shuffled his feet and said impatiently, 'Better get movin', Creek – there she is.'

The man inclined his head and said to Carmody, 'Hear that whistle? Well, you ain't gonna need no horse – because when that train pulls outta here you're gonna be on her. Booth kinda took a dislike to you yesterday so he sent us boys in to

41

see if we couldn't talk you into movin' on. He thought it'd be nice if you left on the same train you came in on this time yesterday. I don't reckon you'll mind leavin' – you must've seen about all there is to see here in twenty-four hours anyway.'

'You tell your boss I'm real touched. Not every stranger'd get a sendoff like this. Only there's just one drawback.'

Creekmore grinned. 'Yes, what's that? No brass band?'

'No. I just ain't about to leave.'

The train whistled again, still distant but drawing steadily nearer. Hallstead urged, 'You'd better get a move on, I'm tellin' you, Creek. If he ain't on that rattler Booth's gonna raise hell.'

'He'll be on it,' Creekmore said quietly. 'In a coffin or out of it maybe – but he'll be on it.'

Carmody drew his shirtsleeve across his mouth and found it strangely dry despite his profuse sweating. He wished he could remember the layout of the buildings and the street behind him. But he couldn't turn to look now. If the shooting started he might have time to drop one of them and jump around the corner and find something, the corner of the boardwalk, anything, to give him cover. Here in this narrow alley it would be like shooting a fish in a barrel when they threw down on him.

'All right, Creekmore – suppose you try to put me on it,' he said.

There was something – maybe the slight change of expression on Creekmore's face, or the flicker of his eyes as they left Carmody's face for an instant – that should have given it away. But it only puzzled him for a split second, and when he caught on it was too late. He saw the shadow of the fifth man against the building as he came up from behind. Saw the upraised gun descending, butt first, and he tried to move aside. Then the train whistled again and and seemed to keep on whistling louder and louder as it plunged into a long dark

42

tunnel with a roar, dragging him with it.

Creekmore bent over the unconscious Carmody, peering down at his face. 'You hit him purty hard, Neaf,' he said laconically.

Neaf Hacker holstered his gun and shrugged. 'Hell, I only tapped him.'

'Well,' said Creekmore, straightening, 'let's pick him up and get him down to the depot. By the time he comes to he'll be halfway to Arizona.'

'How you gonna get him on the train?' Hallstead asked. 'Somebody's gonna kick up a row when they see that knot behind his ear. They ain't gonna let him on like that in case he dies.'

The train whistled again, plainer now, and Creekmore frowned, glancing at Hallstead. 'You think of these things at the damndest time.'

'Yeah, but he's dead right,' Neaf Hacker said, chewing on a match. 'Them train people'll get mighty suspicious.'

Creekmore rubbed his chin reflectively for a second. Then he chuckled. 'I got an idea. Pick him up and let's get him over behind Joe Farwell's barber shop.'

Hacker looked at him blankly. 'I don't get it, Creek.'

'Farwell's got a sideline to his barbershop, ain't he? Now do you get it?'

'Sideline? You mean his undertakin' business? How's that gonna. . . .' Hacker stopped. Then he began to laugh and the others joined in. 'By damn, Creek – you're a card. I'd never have thought of that. Put him in one of Joe's coffins, huh? And load him on the train like. . . .'

Creekmore made an impatient motion. 'Well, let's go or we won't make it. Slip him in a coffin and bring him on down to the depot – and when you get there, don't say nothin'. I'll go on down there right now and fix it up with the station agent to get him aboard. Remember, now – let me do all the talkin'.'

While Creekmore set off for the depot at a fast walk the

43

other four picked up the unconscious Carmody between them and came out from between the buildings.

Down at the depot a long-faced Creekmore was explaining things to the station agent.

'. . . so Booth figgered the decent thing to do was ship the body back to the boy's mother in Amarillo.'

The agent looked up and saw four men bearing a coffin toward the depot, a lazy cloud of dust hanging in their wake as they shuffled along with their burden. 'What'd you say his name was?' he asked.

'Armitage,' Creekmore said quickly. 'Bud Armitage. Amarillo.'

'Strange. Never heard that name around here.'

'Uh – he ain't been with the outfit long. 'Bout a month or so. Just a kid. Allus talkin' about his maw down in Amarillo and how he ought to go back to her.' He took off his hat as the Anvil riders lowered the coffin onto the platform, glowering at them until they caught on and removed theirs.

The station agent sighed and reached through the window for a red flag. 'I'll have to hold up the train. I wish you could've got him in here a little earlier.'

'Did the best we could,' Creekmore said gruffly. Neaf Hacker was seized with a sudden fit of coughing and had to retire around a corner of the depot. The others turned away to hide their grins.

The station agent continued waving the flag at the approaching train until a blast from the whistle told him the engineer had seen it. The train clamoured and clanged to a stop beside the platform. After the explanations had been made and the coffin was being lifted into the baggage car Creekmore said sadly, 'So long, Bud. I reckon you'll get to see your maw sooner'n you thought after all.'

Carmody regained consciousness with a full awareness of a throbbing ache in his head that seemed to be growing worse and threatening to shake him to pieces. He realized from the sounds that he must be on a train, and the pitch blackness and feeling of near-suffocation told him he was in some confined space, probably a wooden box from the smell of it. He was bound and firmly gagged, which added to his discomfort immeasurably.

As his eyes accustomed themselves to the darkness he could see a faint line of light coming from around the lid of the box and he raised himself painfully as far as he could, knowing there would be a certain amount of air coming through the crack. But before he raised his head very far he cracked it on the lid and realized that the box was actually a coffin. With his breathing growing rapidly more difficult he realized that he was using up the air faster that it could be replaced through the crack in the lid; and he knew that unless he got out soon the threat of suffocation would become a reality and the coffin would be the one he would be buried in.

Voices came suddenly through the crack as the door to the baggage car opened and someone entered. He tried to kick his feet to attract attention, but the confined space plus the ropes around his ankles made it impossible for him to do more than slide his bootheels a few inches. A minute later the lid of the coffin creaked and the thin line of light disappeared completely as someone sat down on top of him.

'You oughtn't to sit on a coffin like that, Slim,' the brakeman said reprovingly to the conductor.

'What's wrong with it? He's dead, ain't he? He ain't likely to take no offence.'

The brakeman shrugged. 'All right, have it your way. But it just don't seem decent somehow.'

Inside the coffin Carmody struggled feebly against his bonds, trying to make some noise that would attract their attention before it was too late. But the narrow coffin permitted limited movement and the scuffing sounds he made were lost in the general clatter of the train. He gave up after a while and lay back exhausted. Then the thought came to him that he could make a louder noise by banging his forehead against the lid. But his breathing was growing steadily more laboured, his strength ebbing. The exertion it would require might hasten his own end. He debated waiting until the train stopped. The noise would be more likely to be heard then. On the other hand the two men would most likely leave the baggage car at any stop and his pounding would be in vain. He decided to gather his strength for one final effort.

'You're just superstitious,' the conductor was saying. 'What harm's gonna come from sittin' on a pine box with a dead body in it? A dead human ain't no more alive than a dead horse or any other animal.' Then he chuckled and added, 'Less'n you believe in haunts.'

'Well – I dunno,' the brakeman said cautiously. 'Some funny things happen sometimes when you don't show proper respect for the dead.'

The conductor was still chuckling at this when his friend saw a changed expression come over his face. 'What's the matter,' the brakeman asked the man on the box, 'somethin' wrong?'

'Must've run over a loose rail back there,' the conductor said uneasily. 'Felt the train give a kind of jolt or two.'

'I didn't feel nothin', Slim,' the brakeman said ominously. His eyes lowered themselves to stare at the box on which his friend was sitting.

'Reckon your friend's comin' back to raise nick about me sittin' on him?' he laughed. But the laugh sounded forced and he glanced down at the coffin and laid one hand tentatively on the lid. Suddenly he jumped up and stood back, staring down at it.

'Wh-what's wrong?' the brakeman asked again.

'Why – I dunno.' The conductor swallowed hard. 'I could've sworn that box moved.'

They looked at each other. 'Maybe – maybe it just ain't

sittin' level,' the brakeman suggested hopefully.

'No, that ain't it. It didn't move like that. There was a bump – I felt it when I put my hand on the lid. Like – *like whoever's in there is tryin' to get out.*'

'Oh Lordy!' the brakeman whispered. 'That's what comes of you sittin' on him. His spirit's protestin'. I told you you hadn't ought. . . .'

'Spirit, hell!' the conductor said. 'I ain't talkin' about spooks. You remember them cowhands who put this coffin aboard back at Sand Valley? Recollect how funny they acted?'

'Well – maybe they was just upset about shippin' their friend home.'

'I don't mean that,' the conductor said, advancing toward the coffin. 'There's somethin' funny goin' on here.' He raised his fist and held it poised undecidely above the lid. Then he rapped twice sharply.

Inside, Carmody heard it. With his last remaining ounce of strength he gathered himself and, gritting his teeth against the aching throb in his head, banged his forehead twice against the lid. Then his breath failed him and he slumped back into unconsciousness.

'Hear that!' the conductor said excitedly. 'Somebody's in there – alive. Where's that clawhammer?'

The conductor found the clawhammer and knelt on the coffin. He inserted the hammer claws under the edge of the lid and pried it up. Finally the conductor dropped the hammer and stood up, pulling the lid aside. He reached down, hesitated, then touched Carmody's hand. His eyes widened and he glanced at the brakeman. 'He's warm! Wait – I can feel his heartbeat! He's – *he's alive!*'

CHAPTER 6

The grey fingers of a new day were feeling their way over the eastern horizon when Carmody arrived back in Sand Valley. He had spent most of the previous night asleep on a hard depot bench in a godforsaken spot called Bald Mesa Junction, awaiting an early train which would carry him back. As the hours had slowly ticked away his anger had cooled down through all the successive stages from red-hot fury to a slow boil and finally settled into a kind of cold and controlled rage which was the most dangerous stage of all. It was in this state that he stepped down from the train in the chill light of dawn and strode quickly across the depot platform and up the street toward Buckley's livery.

It took him ten full minutes of pounding and yelling to wake up Buckley who sleepily and grumblingly opened the stables and fitted him out with a mount and saddle.

Caleb was just combing his hair in the cracked mirror outside the bunkhouse door when Carmody splashed across the creek and galloped toward him. Anne heard the clatter of hoofbeats and when she saw who it was she ran out of the house.

'Where the devil you been?' Caleb asked when he dismounted, and Anne stood looking at him anxiously while she waited for him to answer.

Carmody told them, with a laugh or two, about his trip in the coffin.

Anne caught the tenor of his voice and knew the laughs were meant to cover his anger. 'What are you going to do, Jeff?' she said.

'Has Mose Dalmas been here yet?'

'No. Why – is he coming?'

'He said he'd come out and "investigate" and then drop by and let you know what he'd decided.'

Anne sighed. 'Well, I know what that means.' She glanced at Carmody. 'So you're going to wait till he gets here and then tell him what happened to you, is that it?'

Carmody shook his head. 'No, Ma'am. I went to see him on your business and because that was the way you wanted it done. But this is my own private fight and I'll handle it without any hindrance from Mose Dalmas.'

The tall cottonwoods along the creek were throwing long afternoon shadows when Caleb tapped Carmody on the shoulder and pointed. Carmody turned and his eyes followed the pointing finger. A rider had crested the distant rise and was coming at a gentle lope down the long slope toward the valley floor.

'That's him,' Caleb said. 'That's Mose Dalmas.'

Carmody sauntered over to the yard gate and gazed at the approaching rider. Anne came out of the house and stood beside him while Caleb stopped a little distance away. Nobody spoke, but each felt the significance of the silence as they watched the sheriff canter across the flat toward the house.

The sheriff pulled up and dismounted, draping his reins over the gate. He touched his hatbrim and said, 'Afternoon, Anne. Howdy Caleb.' Then he gave Carmody a brief nod and turned back to Anne. 'Hot day for ridin'.'

Dalmas went on, 'I investigated about them steers of yours.'

'Yes?' Anne said expectantly.

Dalmas hooked his thumbs in his gunbelt and rocked back and forth on his heels. 'Well – you know my reputation for

49

honesty and fair play, Anne. I know this is a ticklish situation, you and him bein' close neighbours and all. Now – I had a long talk with Booth and he's been pretty decent about it. He's agreed to forget about the whole thing if you're willing to promise to keep your cows from strayin' onto Anvil territory. Now. . . .'

Anne drew her breath sharply. 'Keep my cows. . . ?' she began. 'What about the four he shot yesterday?' she said angrily.

The sheriff raised a hand and smiled placatingly. 'Now just a minute, Anne. Let's don't get too excited about this. I know how you feel, and in a way I don't blame you for bein' upset. But we got to consider Booth's legal position. Now, he keeps his range fenced. And none of his cows get through that fence onto your range – ain't that right?'

'That's because the gully is too steep from above and. . . .'

'Don't make no difference,' the sheriff said, shaking his head calmly. 'The fact is his cows don't go through that fence. Yours do. And he's got his range posted with keep out notices – that puts you in the position of lettin' your cows trespass on his range. Now. . . .'

'Only trouble there, sheriff,' Carmody cut in quietly, 'is that our cows can't read.'

Dalmas swung on him angrily. 'You keep out of this, *Carmody*,' he said, emphasizing the right name.

Carmody felt that he might have guessed it would come like this. But it had been unexpected all the same. He could feel Anne looking at him, but he didn't turn to look at her.

The sheriff was grinning triumphantly. 'I knowed I'd seen you before somewhere. You've changed some in eight years – but not enough to fool me with a name like Connelly. I dug back in my records after you'd gone yesterday and found out who you was.' He turned to Anne and went on. 'You didn't know who he was, did you, Anne? Well, now you know. I got no notion as to what he's up to, and I can't touch him right now because he's served his sentence. But if I was you I'd get rid of him now that you know.' He touched his hat. 'Well, I got to get back to town. If I can be of any more help to you, Anne, just let me know.'

Nobody noticed or even cared that Dalmas had gone. Anne was standing thunderstruck, staring at Carmody. Carmody was staring straight ahead at nothing, his jaw set resignedly. Caleb stood watching them both, afraid to move.

She was the first to break the silence after a long time. '*You?*' she said in a strained voice that was little more than a whisper. There was no hatred in it. Not yet. Only the shock of sudden discovery.

Carmody turned slowly to look at her, his face solemn. 'Yes, my name's Jeff Carmody,' he said quietly. 'But I didn't kill your husband.'

She shook her head. 'I don't believe you,' she said bitterly. 'You were tried by a jury and found guilty.'

'The jury believed what Mose Dalmas wanted them to believe,' Carmody cut in. 'I heard the shot and rode up to find Clint dead. Dalmas heard it, too, and found me bending over him when he got there. I was going through Clint's pockets, looking for some kind of identification. Dalmas said I was robbing him. I was a stranger passing through. Dalmas had to pin it on somebody and I happened to be handy. It saved him the trouble of trying to find the man who *did* do it.'

Anne stared at him. 'Why did you come back here?'

'I spent eight years in prison for another man's crime,' Carmody said quietly. 'I came back to find him.'

She watched him silently for a long time. 'I don't believe you,' she said again. 'I think your conscience drove you back here when you heard the man you killed had left a wife and baby. Well, that's small credit to you, Jeff Carmody. But I don't want your help.' Her voice lowered, hoarse with emotion. 'Now get out of here.'

'He didn't do it, Anne,' Caleb said gently. 'He didn't kill Clint.'

51

She swung to face him. 'Can you prove he didn't?' she said sharply.

Caleb shook his head slowly. 'No, I can't prove it, Anne,' he said quietly. ' 'Cept I know he didn't. He just ain't that kind. You can tell by lookin' at him.'

For a minute she looked at him and said nothing. Then she laughed, a laugh that was little more than an hysterical sob. 'You old fool! You'd like for me to believe you, wouldn't you? You'd like for me to keep him around so that every day I'd be tortured with wondering whether or not I was keeping the man who'd killed my husband.'

The old man's eyes widened and he started to speak but she cut him off. 'Oh, don't look so surprised,' she said with a bitter smile. 'I'm not blind, Caleb. Don't you think I could see how you've hated me from the first moment Clint brought me here? You were happy with him until I came into his life. You felt I had no right to share his companionship after all the years you'd known him. God knows why you've stayed with me – unless it was to enjoy seeing me suffer. And now you want me to keep a man who killed my husband, just because I need help against Anson. You'd enjoy that even more, wouldn't you, Caleb?'

Her voice caught in a sob and she leaned against the gate for support while Carmody and the old man watched her helplessly. She lifted her face and it was streaked with tears. 'Get out!' she whispered. 'Get out – *both of you!*'

Carmody hesitated, then turned slowly away. Anne pushed herself away from the fence and started blindly for the house. Caleb watched her, then turned and shuffled slowly towards the bunkhouse, his old face sad, his head bowed. Anne paused, watching him go. Then she called, 'Caleb!' and rushed up to him and he caught her while she buried her face on his shoulder, sobbing. 'Caleb, I didn't mean it! I didn't mean what I said. You've been . . . so good to me. . . .' She began to cry quietly and the old man raised his eyes to meet

Carmody's across the yard. 'You'd better go, Jeff,' he said quietly. 'Maybe this'll blow over one day.'

Carmody turned away and went thoughtfully to the bunkhouse where he rolled his blankets and picked up his few belongings and stuffed them in his warbag. As he was tying them behind his saddle Penelope came up to him holding the pup in her arms. 'Why is Mommy crying, Jeff?' she asked.

Carmody glanced down at her. Then he smiled and ruffled her hair. 'Because she's a woman, I guess,' he said with a sigh and mounted up.

The little girl's eyes lighted on the warbag. 'Are you going away, Jeff?'

He nodded.

'But you'll come back?'

Carmody set his jaw, looking across the yard to where Caleb was helping Anne into the house. 'Sure, little lady,' he promised. 'I'll come back.' He lifted his hand and gave her a bright smile, then reined his mount around and set off through the cottonwoods and across the creek.

He rode aimlessly for a while, sunk deep in gloomy thought. He had handled it all wrong from the start, he thought. Maybe he should have made a clean breast of it from the beginning, even to Mose Dalmas. At least that would have prevented Dalmas from using the knowledge as a weapon. But would it have made any difference with Anne? He doubted it, remembering the look in her eyes when she had talked about the man she still believed to be in prison. But she had accused him of coming back to help her to salve his conscience. At least that was something, she gave him credit for having one.

Her outburst at Caleb puzzled him more than a little. She was damned lucky, the way he figured, to have the old man stick with her like he had. At Caleb's age a man liked to look forward to a few last years of peace and quiet; not trying to battle against odds for a headstrong young widow. He thought of her remark about Caleb hating her for taking Clint's companionship away from him. That could have been mostly imagination. From what he had heard of women they were apt to be jealous of their husbands' love. Especially a woman like her who had been kicked around until Clint took her away. But most likely it had been her imagination and the outburst had been purely emotional. She had regretted it right away and apologized to Caleb. And the poor old boy had looked plain stunned when she had flung the accusation at him.

Well – one thing would clear the air all round. Find the man who had killed Clint Merriweather. He felt his pocket to make sure the rowel was still there, and he smiled grimly. '. . . *there's maybe sixty thousand men in the State of Texas wears spurs.*' Still, it was a hope. The only hope he had – so he clung to it.

The sight of the Anvil fence stirred him from his thoughts. A hundred yards away was a gap-gate and he rode toward it, his eyes searching the area just beyond the fence. He dismounted and lifted the wire loop from the post and held it aside while he led his mount through, then turned to fasten it, glancing idly at the sign that said, ANVIL RANCH. BOOTH ANSON PROP. KEEP OUT! He had his toe in the stirrup to mount again when a voice from the mesquite behind said lazily, 'S'matter, fella, can't you read?'

Without taking his foot from the stirrup Carmody turned to look over his shoulder. Neaf Hacker stood there. Hallstead was with him. His eyes flicked to the brush and he wondered how many more lay hidden.

'Nope,' he said casually. 'I never learned my ABC's. Why, what's that sign say?'

'It says keep out, that's what it says.'

'Good idea,' Carmody nodded solemnly. 'Otherwise you might get all sorts of folks comin' in here.'

Hacker took an angry step forward, stiff-legged, arms at his sides. Hallstead's hand rested on his gun butt, waiting. 'You're real smart, ain't you, Carmody?'

'I see the word's got around. Mose Dalmas must've told you.'

Hacker looked puzzled. 'About you actin' smart?'

'No. Anybody can just tell by lookin' at me how smart I am. I mean about my name. What else did Mose tell you?' Carmody was talking for time. He knew that to try to mount would invite a bullet; and in that awkward position, with his right leg in the air, he wouldn't have a prayer. But to put his foot down would be to take a stand against odds. Either way it would be rough.

'He told Booth that nobody has a right to trespass on private property. And that's what you're doin' right now.' Hacker grinned confidently, knowing he had made Carmody's position clear. 'This time,' he added pointedly, 'you're gonna stay in your coffin.'

At the word 'coffin' Hallstead commenced his draw and Hacker's right hand blurred into motion. Carmody jerked his left foot from the stirrup, firing as he spun around. Hacker and Hallstead were already wreathed in gunsmoke which jerked and eddied as they thumbed shot after shot. Carmody's first shot missed completely but his second took Hallstead full in the chest, sending him backward with a grunt under the impact of the heavy slug. A bullet whispered in Carmody's ear and he heard the clang of iron as it riccocheted off the horn of the saddle behind his head. Something lunged into him suddenly from behind and the frenzied whinny of pain told him the livery mount had been mortally stricken. He leapt aside to avoid the thrashing hoofs as the animal went down, still firing at Hacker as he moved. Hacker dropped his gun and screamed, clutching at his lower belly as he staggered forward through his own gunsmoke, his eyes wide with pain and fear as he realized he was dying. He stumbled to his knees, doubling forward in agony, the blood dribbling between his clasped fingers. Carmody lowered his gun slowly and watched the man slump forward in the dust where he struggled convulsively for an instant and then lay still.

Carmody walked over to the dead Hacker and stood above him for a minute. Bending down he jerked one of the man's boots straight and glanced at the spur. It was hand-hammered Mexican brass with inch and a half Chihuahua rowel. He let the boot drop and walked over to Hallstead and made a similar examination. This time he found long-shanked blued steel with small star rowels of the professional bronc-stomper.

He stood up and glanced around. They must have mounts here, he thought. He found them and brought them out, trussing the bodies face down over one of the protesting horses. Then he stripped the saddle from the dead livery animal and cached it in the mesquite. Mounting the remaining horse he dropped a loop around the dead one's hindlegs and dragged it out of sight. Then he came back and taking the corpses in tow, set off deeper into Anvil territory.

The trail led him as he thought it would, to Anson's head-quarters. He drew rein at the head of the valley where a stand of twisted cedar offered cover. Dismounting, he squatted to roll a cigarette while he looked the situation over.

There was little visible activity among the buildings and corrals below. He guessed, and rightly, that the main force of Anvil hands would be away on routine jobs. But a glance at the sun told him it was nearing noon. The question was whether the riders would be too far away to ride back for their midday meal. He decided to wait a little while.

The ring of a triangle sounding the noon meal call reached his ears. A solitary hand came out of one of the outbuildings, dropped a handful of tools on a bench and walked toward the cook shack wiping his hands on his pants. Carmody watched for others but none came and he judged that the man he had seen, plus the cook, must be the only help around.

His eyes shifted to the main house. The question now was whether Booth Anson himself was home. Carmody decided there was but one way to find out. He ground his cigarette under his boot and remounted, riding warily down the slope. Without incident he reached the white slab fence surrounding the yard and dismounted, leaving both horses at the hitchrack.

Hand on gun, Carmody went carefully up the steps, eyeing the open windows on either side of the door. On the verandah he paused, listening for small sounds above the thumping of his heart. A shuffling of stabled horses came from beyond the house. But the house itself lay quiet.

Through the door ahead he could look the length of the hall. It was empty except for a buffalo horn hatrack, a hide-covered chair and a leather-bound trunk. He glanced again at the windows on either side. The room on the right was furnished as a dining room with heavily-carved Victorian rosewood table, chair and sideboard. He moved silently to the left, keeping close to the wall as he peered inside. This would be Anson's office, he judged. A big mahogany desk was heaped with an assortment of litter. The rest of the room was in keeping, from the scuffed shotgun chaps hung from a hook beside the stone fireplace to the stirrup-less saddle gathering dust in a corner.

He started with the desk, sifting quickly through the litter on top until it occurred to him that eight years would be a long time to leave a pair of spurs lying on top of a desk, even one as disorderly as this. He tried the drawers. Until he reached the bottom one on the left his search netted him nothing but the usual collection of junk he might be expected to find in a cattleman's desk. Tally sheets and partially-filled ledgers dating consecutively from 1870 to 1885 were there. He glanced briefly at the tally sheets, raising his eyebrows at the yearly increases they showed. Anson didn't need more land, and even if his present water supply was precarious, he was doing all right. But Carmody reminded himself he hadn't come to snoop into Anson's business and he put the sheets away and turned his attention to a locked bottom drawer.

There were several rusty keys in the big drawer above. He

tried them all without success. Then he rubbed his chin while he contemplated breaking it open. Would a man lock a pair of spurs with a missing rowel away in a drawer? Not likely. Unless Anson had a strong hunch what had happened to the missing rowel and wanted to keep them out of sight.

He tested the drawer again, making certain it wasn't just stuck. Then he glanced around the room until he found a sheath knife hanging from a peg. When he finally got it open he was disappointed. A small japanned cash box was all it held. It was unlocked. A heavy sheet of paper, folded over and over again, filled the box. It looked like a map. He drew it out and saw he was right.

Unfolding it he caught a glimpse of place names that were unfamiliar; names of creeks and canyons and trails. It was a government survey map dated 1860. A winding line in faded blue at the bottom of the page was marked 'Canadian River' in crudely-inked letters. Then he took a closer look at the map and saw a square labelled 'Sand Valley, est. 1868.' After that it began to make more sense.

An area covering four sections at the eastern edge was marked, 'Anvil Range, 1865.' Each year after that the growth of Anson's empire was recorded, dated lines marking the new Anvil borders haphazardly as his cattle spread out over open range. The coming of barbed wire and the end of the old open range straightened the haphazard boundaries with such notations as 'Fenced, 1872.'

Carmody noticed several smaller areas identified with what must have been the former owners' names before the Anvil began to spread. These names had been crossed out, with the date noted. Only three that he could find were marked, 'bought'. The rest, maybe a dozen in all, were blandly labelled, 'acquired'. Four of these had tiny skulls and cross-bones drawn in after the owners' struck-out names. Carmody could guess their meaning easily enough.

Between the eastern and western divisions of Anson's Anvil

empire was driven a solid wedge five sections long running from north to south and a section wide. This was the Merriweather place, and Carmody found a variety of notations here. The most prominent was marked, 'NEXT!' But the last item he noticed proved to be most important of all.

Along the stage road between Canadian and Sand Valley at the point where Carmody had found Clint Merriweather's body on that fateful night was an X-mark. Beside it were these words: 'Clint Merriweather killed here night of June 12, 1877 by persons unknown.'

At first it didn't sink in. Then Carmody read it again and the words jumped out at him. '. . . *by persons unknown.*' He raised his eyes slowly and stared at the opposite wall without seeing it while the meaning took effect.

Booth Anson had not killed Clint! Otherwise why had he bothered to make a point of saying, '. . . by persons unknown?' There was no skull and crossbones here as with the other names – and Jeff was certain that the significance was plain. Anson kept the map locked up, so obviously he had no intention of it ever becoming public. Then why bother to make that remark about 'persons unknown' unless Anson was genuinely in doubt?

If this reasoning was right, one other conclusion became obvious to Carmody. *Anson knew that Carmody had not killed Clint Merriweather.*

But how?

Carmody glanced at the words again, a puzzled frown wrinkling his brow. Then he folded it thoughtfully and put it back in its box and closed the drawer, working the lock up with the point of the knife until it would require a key to open it.

The sudden distant clatter of hoofbeats brought Carmody out of his thoughts into reality. He crossed to the window and glanced out. Anvil riders, half a dozen of them, were crossing the valley floor toward the house at a dust-raising gallop. Carmody recognized Anson well in the lead on a mouse-coloured gelding.

The reason for the riders' haste was pretty plain. From the crest of the rise above the valley they had seen the horses in front of the house, and even at that distance there was no mistaking that those were dead men draped over the back of one.

Carmody stepped back from the window and glanced around. There was no point in trying to run out now. Besides, he had come here purposely to see Booth Anson. Well, here was his chance. But, he figured glumly, he had counted on seeing him a little more privately than this. He pulled his hat down firmly and tested his Colt in its holster to make sure it rode free. Then he said aloud, 'Boy, you ain't gonna talk your way of this, Carmody!' With a deep sigh he stepped through the hall and out onto the verandah. He stood on the top step just as Anson and the others pulled up at the gate in a cloud of dust and sat staring in angry silence at the bodies.

Creekmore nudged Anson and said something, nodding toward the verandah. Anson jerked his head around, saw Carmody lounging against the pillar. With a curse he jumped to the ground. There was a rattle and squeak of gear as his crew followed. Anson strode up to the gate, slammed it open and took two strides up the gravelled path and stopped, hand on his gun.

'What the hell's this all about?' he roared.

Carmody was fashioning a cigarette with a calmness he knew was pure sham. He struck a match with his thumbnail, surprised at the steadiness of his hand. There are six men down there, he thought, surveying the group over the flare of the match. One for every shell in his gun. Even if they stood still and let him pot shoot he knew he'd be lucky to get them all.

He flipped the match carelessly away and indicated the bodies with a nod of his head. 'Them the best gun hands you got to offer, Anson?' he said with a grin.

The sheer brass of it brought a stunned silence for a second. That one man should cut down Hacker and Hallstead and then bring the bodies in while he faced six others and laughed in their face . . . Carmody was banking heavily on the notion that the two had been Anson's best. It was likely that they had been put on the fence, knowing Carmody would come here after the sheriff's visit, and they had been put there in full confidence that they would stop Carmody without effort.

He saw now as he watched the reaction on the faces before him that his hunch was right. And he decided to push his advantage – because it was his only hope. Already the effect was beginning to wear – one or two men glancing uncertainly at Anson, their hands moving furtively toward their guns.

'Before any of you gents get the notion you'd like to try your luck with a gun,' he said quietly, 'I'll tell you straight I'll put a bullet through the head of the first man who tries. And just in case you think I'm kiddin', it ain't been half an hour since I told the same thing to them two draped across that horse. Take a look at them and decide if you'd like to try.'

This was the moment of decision, he knew. The next few seconds would see him in complete command of the situation or lying bullet-riddled and broken on the steps. He saw Anson glaring at him, knew the man was remembering their first encounter when, unarmed, he had ripped him saddle and all from his horse. He had not been bluffing then, he could read the uncertainty in Anson's glance now that he was armed.

The proof of the bluff was there on the horses. He saw the men turn their heads to look again. Saw the uneasiness come over them at the sight of Hallstead's upside-down face staring unseeing at them, caked blood matting the nostrils and down-hanging hair. Tensed fingers relaxed away from gun butts; eyes shifted to meet his with a look of mingled hatred and respect, then moved questioningly to Anson's face.

With a surge of relief Carmody felt the moment had passed.

But he still had a long way to go.

'He's bluffin'!' Anson growled. 'Creek, Gillman – and you others. Spread along the fence and get ready to back me. Hell, he's only one man!'

Carmody saw them shuffle a little. Packed like this, bunched at the gate, he had better control. If they spread out. . . .

'First man moves . . . he's dead meat!' Carmody said unhurriedly.

'Creek! Gillman! Hell's the matter with you guys?' Anson's voice took on a note of desperation. 'You afraid of him?'

Creekmore shrugged. 'Hell no . . . but then I don't reckon Hacker or Hallstead was either. This ain't the time, Booth. There'll come another.'

'From the back maybe, Creekmore?' Carmody said.

The man gave an ugly smile. 'That's your lookout, sonny,' he said softly.

Anson snorted at his foreman. 'So that's what I pay you for, huh? To make smart talk.'

'You want to call his bluff, Booth?' Creekmore asked quietly. 'You go ahead – I'll back you up. But you just go ahead first.'

For a minute Carmody thought Anson was mad enough to try. But the Anvil owner dropped his gun hand, shoulders limp. He looked at Carmody. 'Now – if it ain't askin' too much, what the hell're you doin' here, Carmody?'

Carmody's attention was on Anson, but he knew Creekmore would be waiting the chance. Carmody's eyes had barely shifted to Anson's face when he sensed, rather than saw, that Creekmore was starting his draw.

One minute Carmody was indolently lounging; the next instant he had thrust his shoulder away from the post and his gun had exploded in his hand.

Astonishment made a stricken grimace on Creekmore's face as the slug slammed him backwards into the man behind him. His body jerked to the impact, his hand let the Colt drop back into leather before it was fully clear. For a second he seemed to hang backwards on his heels, stiffening, then he collapsed into a heap on the gravel.

There was a moment of stunned silence during which the Anvil crew stared at the gunsmoke wreathing the man on the porch as if wondering where it had come from.

'Anybody else want to try their luck?' Carmody said softly.

Nobody moved. Nobody spoke.

Carmody straightened a little, gesturing with his Colt. 'Just to make sure you ain't tempted, suppose you all unharness.'

There was another sigh from Anson as the man fought his pride and frustration with common sense. 'I don't know what you come here for, mister, but I do know this much – when you leave you'd better keep movin'. 'Cause if I ever catch sight of you in Hemphill County again I'm gonna nail your hide to the barn door, and I don't give a damn how I do it – I'll bushwack you, I'll backshoot you, I'll do any damn thing I have to. But I'll get you.'

'Like you got Myers and Stalton and Sands and Brewer?' Carmody said.

Anson shot him a curious look. These were names Carmody had picked off the map. Names of small outfits, little ranchers or nesters which had been crossed off and replaced by small skulls and crossbones.

'Who's spreadin' that kind of talk?' Anson said, eyes narrowing. 'Just because I take over abandoned range when a man dies ain't no sign I killed him.'

'If any spreadin' been done, you've done it yourself,' Carmody said. 'You built your own reputation for being a pusher, nobody else. But there comes a time you meet somebody you can't push.'

'You speakin' for yourself – or for Widow Merriweather?'

'Maybe a little of both, Anson. Which brings me around to why I bothered to come here in the first place – now step away

63

from them gunbelts, all of you, and let's go inside to your office, Anson. I had aimed to talk this over with you in private, but you don't leave me much choice.' He wagged the gun impatiently, 'Come on – all five of you. Inside. There's plenty of room.'

Anson shoved his hands through his trouser belt and spread his feet defiantly. 'You done enough orderin' around, Carmody. I ain't bein' pushed around my own place. Speak your piece and then get the hell. . . .'

He left the sentence unfinished, throwing up his arms to protect his face from flying gravel as the slug from Carmody's Colt ripped the ground at his feet and whined away in riccochet. 'I'm callin' the tune right now, Anson. You do the dancin'.'

Anson shoved past him, glowering belligerently. Carmody covered them as they passed into the house, standing where he could watch both the length of the hall and Anson's office as they filed in. When they were all in the room Carmody joined them.

Carmody sat on a corner of the desk, facing them. For some reason he felt nervous, uneasy. He didn't know why. The worst was over – but maybe that was it. His nerves had been stretched fiddle tight out there on the steps and now the let-down was setting in. To keep up a show of calm he plucked a cheroot from the box on Anson's desk and bit off the end.

'I said I wanted just two things from you Anson, sixty-four dollars for them four steers of Anne Merriweather's, and an apology for shovin' me on that train yesterday.'

Anson thrust his head forward like a bull, tendons straining again his shirt collar. 'You can fiddle for both your sixty-four dollars and your apology – 'cause you ain't getting a nickel or spit outta me!'

Carmody reached down with his left hand and gripped a corner of the desk. 'Real heavy, ain't it?' he smiled.

'Mahogany. Y'know something, Anson – down in Huntsville they had me bustin' granite boulders with a sixteen pound sledge. After eight years of that a man gets a powerful amount of strength in his arms. Now – the question is, are you gonna tell me I can have that sixty-four dollars, or am I gonna have to tear this place apart to find it?'

'You can go straight to. . . !'

Carmody gripped the desk with one hand before Anson finished and flipped it, gritting his teeth at the strain of the weight. It somersaulted into the fireplace with a crash that shook the room. The top split, drawers spewed open, their contents cascading across the floor.

'I don't see any money in there,' Carmody said easily. 'But that'll be nice when the weather gets cold this fall – all you'll have to do is toss a match to her and away she goes.'

'Damn you, Carmody! That desk cost me two hundred dollars to freight out here from Chicago!'

'You gonna get that sixty-four dollars – or do I start on the floor puncheons next?' He nodded toward the fireplace. 'Your cash wouldn't be in that little japanned box I see there, would it?'

Anson's anger faded quickly. 'Why – no, it ain't,' he said, suddenly meek. 'That's just some personal papers – all right, I'll get your damn money.' He spun on his heel and ripped aside a pile of hides in the corner, uncovering a tiny safe. As he knelt down to open it Carmody called sharply, 'Hold it, Anson!' and walked across to him. 'It ain't no secret that folks sometimes keep a gun in a safe,' he smiled. 'Unlock it and then step back.'

While Anson fumbled with the safe Carmody glanced at the spurs the man wore and was disappointed. Long-shanked gun steel with a chap guard and one-inch rowels. Good utility hooks they were, but nothing fancy. And though it occurred to him that Anson could have hidden the others or thrown them away, it was a safe bet that the rowel in his pocket had never belonged to Anson.

Anson clicked open the safe and stepped back with an angry gesture. 'All right, Carmody – the money's there. But you can tell that woman boss of yours she made a big mistake sending you here. A mistake she'll regret.'

Carmody hunkered down, watching them, feeling inside the safe till his hand encountered a doeskin bag that chinked when he touched it. He stood up and dumped it on top of the safe saying to Anson, 'She didn't send me. And she's not my boss anymore. Your friend Dalmas fixed that. He told her who I was.'

'And she fired you?'

'I didn't wait around to find out.'

Anson was genuinely curious now. Curious and suspicious. He studied Carmody's face thoughtfully. 'Then what do you want with that money if you don't work for her anymore?'

'It's a kind of a going-away present,' Carmody said with a touch of bitterness.

A voice behind him drawled, 'Then you won't be needin' it, fella – because you ain't goin' noplace. Now drop that cutter and heist your hands 'fore I blast a hole in your backbone.'

The stunned shock of surprise Carmody felt was accompanied by a wave of rage at his own careless stupidity. Now he realized the uneasiness he had felt earlier was due to something he had tried to remember but couldn't quite place in his mind. Now he recalled with sudden clarity the picture he had seen from the top of the ridge – the rider coming from one of the outbuildings in answer to the meal call, laying his tools on a bench and walking toward the cookshack wiping his hand on his thighs.

He felt the vicious dig of the Colt in his back and the man said impatiently, 'Drop it, I said!'

The grin he saw spread across Anson's evil face made things all too clear. The cards were down and he'd bluffed his lean hand for all he could, staking his life on it. And now he was up against Anson's ace in the hole – the man at the back with the gun.

He had a choice. He could drop his gun and let Anson hang him. Or he could turn and fight. Either way he knew he would die. But there would be more satisfaction if he died fighting.

He heard Anson yell, 'Watch him!' as he sidestepped and spun, jerking his Colt around and squeezing the trigger. There were two explosions together and something red-hot struck his chest near his heart with terrific force that shook the wind from him. He had a vague glimpse of his own wild bullet gouging a smoking furrow along the plaster, and he was conscious of acrid gunsmoke burning his eyes as he doubled forward into inky blackness.

The men in the room stared once at Carmody, then relaxed, grinning at the man with the still-smoking gun. Anson shoved back his hat and let out his breath. 'Whew-eee! By God, Troxel, I thought you was never gonna get up here!'

Troxel grunted and said anxiously to a man bending over Carmody, 'Did I get him?'

The other felt Carmody's pulse, then shook his head. 'Naw, he's still alive.'

'Then stand aside,' Troxel said, motioning impatiently with his gun, 'I'll finish him.'

'Hold it, Trox!' Anson said quickly, 'I just thought of somethin'. We can use him.'

Anson glanced down at Carmody, rubbing his chin and smiling faintly. 'Supposin' . . .' he began thoughtfully. 'Supposin' there was to be a couple of raids on the Merriweather place? Who d'you reckon would get the blame?'

'Huh – the way things are between you and her, even old Mose Dalmas'd have to be blind not to see it.'

'But supposin' word got around that Carmody and the gal'd had a fallin' out after she found out who he was? And supposin' on the last raid somebody set fire to the place and killed off Anne and Old Caleb, and Carmody's body was found across the creek with a bullet in it?'

Troxel's face broke in an ugly grin and he lowered his gun. 'I getcha, Booth. You don't need to spell it out – I getcha.'

CHAPTER 7

Carmody came slowly awake in a room that was filled with the grey shadows of twilight. With the gradual return of consciousness came the awareness of a burning pain in his chest that made breathing difficult. It was as if a red hot bar of iron lay across him, pinning him as he lay. He tried to raise his hand to push it away and found he was too weak to move.

A voice called out in the house below, accompanied by a curse, and suddenly the memory of what had happened came back to him with a rush. He remembered the man behind him calling to him to drop his gun; remembered turning to fight it out. Then the crash of the explosions loud in the room and the heavy kick of the slug in his chest. And then the soft blackness.

But he was still alive, and he found that the most surprising thing of all. By rights, Anson should have killed him. He had expected it after what he had done to Hacker, Hallstead and Creekmore. But Anson must have brought him up here to this room for some reason he could not understand.

He raised his head with difficulty and peered down at his chest and noticed that he was in his underwear. There was a jagged rent in his undershirt, stained with dried blood and running horizontally across his chest. There had been no attempt at bandaging. He moved one hand feebly and gingerly touched the edge of the wound. It hurt like hell. The slug must have struck at an angle in the region of his heart as he was turning and gouged its way across his rib cage and out the other side. Weakness got the better of him and he let his head fall back on the bed, sweating profusely with the effort.

It was much later when he was awakened by the sound of footsteps on the stairs. He glanced toward the door and saw the glow of lamplight on the stairway and a man came into the room, hand on his gun as he held the lamp high and peered cautiously at him.

'You finally woke up, huh?' the man said, putting the lamp on the washstand and letting his hand fall away from his gun when he saw there was no danger.

'Don't feel so much like bustin' up the furniture now, eh, Carmody?' The man laughed and tilted the chair back against the wall and sat down to roll a smoke. He glanced at Carmody's bloodstained undershirt then back to his face. 'You're damn lucky at that.'

A voice boomed up the stairs. 'Hey, Vicker! How is he?' Cormody recognized it as Anson's.

Vicker scuffed out of the chair and slouched to the door. 'He's all right, Booth. He just come round. But he ain't feelin' like tearin' the place apart now. He's weaker'n a newborn calf.'

Anson's chuckle floated up. 'Thought that'd take some of the starch out of him. Does he feel like eatin'? There's some grub down in the kitchen if he does. We gotta fatten him up and get him back on his feet.'

Vicker turned to Carmody. 'Feel like eatin', fireball?'

Carmody had never felt less hungry in his life. But he knew he had to get his strength back. 'Sure,' he said feebly, 'I'll eat.'

The man slouched down the stairs and came back in a few minutes with a bowl of stew and a tablespoon. 'You able to sit up?'

Carmody gritted his teeth and pulled himself up on one elbow, dragging himself backwards a little until he could brace himself against the head of the iron bedstead. The exertion broke open the wound and he felt a warm trickle of blood across his belly. Vicker put the bowl on the bed beside him and handed him the spoon. 'Here, you gotta do it yourself. I ain't no nursemaid.'

Carmody refrained from answering, digging at the stew. It smelled pretty good and he decided maybe he could actually enjoy it if the pain didn't bother him too much. He spilled half the first spoonful with his shaky hand and thereafter learned not to fill it so full. When he had finished he dropped the spoon in the bowl with a clatter and slid down in the bed exhausted.

Vicker dropped his chair to the floor and sauntered over to pick up the bowl. 'You did all right for a sick invalid.'

Carmody was glad he'd eaten. Already he felt better for it. He turned his head to look at Vicker. 'Where'd you put my clothes?'

'Clothes?' Vicker laughed. 'Hell, what do you want with clothes? You ain't goin' nowhere.'

'Not now, maybe. But I don't aim to lay here the rest of the summer. Where'd you put 'em?'

Vicker went back to his chair and cocked it against the wall, grinning. 'Well, now – since you ask, maybe I'll let you in on a little secret. We got a use for your duds. And we got a use for you, too, when you get your pins under you again.'

Vicker went on to explain Anson's plan for having a rider harass the Merriweather place dressed in Carmody's clothes. 'There's a good moon these nights. I'm about your build. And after the Merriweather gal throwin' you off her place today, well. . . .' he spread his hands and laughed. 'She'll figure it was you comin' back to get even.'

Carmody turned away and stared at the rim of the moon just peering over the rim of the valley. Then he looked back at his guard. 'You lousy son of a bitch,' he said quietly.

Vicker shook with silent laughter. 'Hell, you ain't heard the best of it. After she's had a few nights of that and word's got in to the sheriff that you're raisin' hell – well, one night there's gonna be a real big raid, with a lot of shootin'. When it's over there ain't gonna be nothin' left of the Merriweather place but ashes. And when old Mose goes pokin' around he's gonna find your carcass right across the creek from the house with a bullet in it. Just like you'd been shot tryin' to burn the place. After that. . . .' he shrugged, '. . . well, you get all the blame, Booth Anson gets the Merriweather place. Simple, ain't it?'

There was silence for a minute in which the two men's eyes met in the glow of the lamp. 'If I could get out of this bed,' Carmody said slowly, 'I'd kick your goddam teeth in.'

Vicker's smile faded and he kicked his chair out from under himself and stood beside the bed. 'Listen, mister,' he said, his breath whistling through his clenched teeth, 'you called me a name a minute ago that no man ever called me and lived. I let it go because you're a sick man. But don't push me, Carmody, or I'll lay your face open with a pistol barrel.'

Anson's voice came urgently up the stairs. 'Vicker! Blow out that lamp and keep an eye on Carmody. There's a rider comin' – looks like it might be the Merriweather gal. If Carmody tries to yell or anythin', slug him.'

'That'd be a pleasure, Booth,' Vicker replied with a look at Carmody. He stepped over to the lamp and cupped his hand over the chimney and blew sharply.

'Just lay quiet, friend,' Vicker warned. 'It's her all right.'

The drone of conversation drifted on the night air. He gathered that Anne was in no immediate danger herself. The tone of Anson's voice told him that. But that was the very thing that roused his suspicion. The man was putting himself out to be polite and Carmody knew there was treachery in the air. He heard his own name mentioned once or twice and that convinced him all the more. If what Vicker had told him already was true, then Anson must be paving the way by acting friendly toward Anne so that the blame would more readily fall on Carmody when the raids came.

He gave serious thought to the idea of calling out to let her know he was here. Then he rejected the notion. In his present weakened state he doubted if his voice would carry sufficiently to be heard beyond the room. And the attempt would be certain to bring swift reprisal from Vicker. Nor would the man be gentle. A crack on the head with a pistol barrel would only delay his recovery. No, what he needed was to regain his strength as rapidly as possible so that he could try to make his escape before Anson pulled the final disastrous raid.

How long would that be, he wondered? At best it would be several days before his body replaced the lost blood and built up enough strength to permit him to stand. He knew that if he could get to his feet he could get to a horse and ride. The question was – would Anson wait that long? The man was not the kind to sit around and risk somebody stumbling onto the fact that Carmody was here. The chances were he would begin the preliminary raids immediately – Vicker had mentioned the 'good moon these nights' and the full moon would grow later and wane with each passing night. It was a safe bet then that as soon as Carmody showed any sign of returning strength. . . .

'Troxel, come on out here!' he heard Anson bellow. There was further noise of boots going down the gravel path and Carmody strained his ears to listen.

Vicker chuckled. 'He's sendin' Troxel to see her home. Booth's bein' plumb neighbourly.'

It was perhaps an hour later, judging from the moon, when he wakened to the thud of boots in the room. A match flared and he saw Vicker light the lamp. Anson was with him.

'Looks like your twin, don't he?' Anson grinned, nodding at Vicker.

Vicker turned in the lamplight and Carmody could see the man was wearing his clothes. 'Hat's a little big,' Vicker complained. 'Had to stuff paper in the sweatband.'

'Didn't figure you'd have brains enough to fill a man's hat,'

73

Carmody said feebly.

Anger flashed in Vicker's eyes and he jerked up his arm to backhand Carmody across the face, but Anson stiff-armed him in the shoulder, shoving him aside. 'Save it!' he growled.

Vicker glowered at him. 'If you want to keep him in one piece you'd better tell him to stop shootin' off his mouth or I'll. . . .'

'I said, save it!' Anson said angrily. 'You didn't have to wait till you got him stretched out in here to show how tough you were – you had a chance to draw on him this afternoon. I didn't notice you actin' so eager then.'

'I don't recollect you shovin' anybody aside to get at him!'

'Ah-h-h!' Anson said with a gesture of derision and turned away to look at Carmody. 'I had a little chat with the Merriweather girl about an hour ago. She asked if I'd seen you and I told her you'd come by this mornin' and tried to hire on with me thinkin' you'd have a chance to get back at her. I said you'd told me you'd waited all those years in the state pen just plannin' how to get even, and that you'd figured on gettin' a job with her so's you could bust her apart slow from the inside.'

Anson chuckled at the look on Carmody's face. 'She seemed right put out about it – especially since she'd come here looking for you so's she could pay you your wages. But I told her I'd chased you off the place. I didn't like to worry her, but I told her you'd likely be back to cause her some trouble, judgin' from the way you'd talked. So' – Anson jerked his thumb to indicate Vicker – 'here you go to chouse a few head of MW beef down across the creek and shoot 'em down in her front yard. We'll try that for two, three nights and then. . . .'

'I heard it all before,' Carmody cut in. 'Now why don't both of you get the hell out of here and let me sleep.'

Anson grinned. 'We will – we only thought you might like somethin' to dream about so we dropped in to tell you.'

'What about the horse, Booth?' Vicker said.

'Oh yeah ... where's that livery nag you was ridin',
Carmody? You come down here today on Hallstead's mount.
What'd you do with yours?'

Carmody thought for a minute, looking at the man. Then
he smiled. 'Afraid Vicker's might get shot out from under him
and leave an Anvil brand behind to be identified ... that's it,
ain't it? Be safer if you had mine, I reckon. Now that's a damn
shame.'

Anson frowned. '*What's* a damn shame?'

Carmody was about to tell him what had happened to the
horse, but checked himself in time. If they knew the dead
horse was so near the fence where Anne might have seen it
and got suspicious ... well, they might not wait for him to get
well. As it was, there was a chance she might have seen it – and
it would tell her Anson had lied. When the raid came tonight
she might guess the truth. Just might. If she didn't discover the
dead horse things would be no worse off than they were now.
But there was no point in giving a helping hand to Anson.

'Why, it's a damn shame I turned him loose. But when I
plugged your two gunslingers up by the fence today I found I
had one horse more'n I needed, so I turned the rented one
loose.'

'I think you're lyin',' Anson said suspiciously.

'Well, you can always ride into Sand Valley and ask Buckley
if it's showed up yet,' Carmody said indifferently.

Vicker suddenly raised a hand and said, 'Listen!' The sound
of rapid hoofbeats rattled a tattoo in the moonlight outside as
a rider crossed the flats toward the house. Vicker went to the
window and looked out. 'It's Trox comin' back.'

'Then come on,' Anson told him. 'You got ridin' to do.'

'What about Carmody's horse?'

'T'hell with it. Take a mount with a blotched brand outta
the corral – we got plenty of 'em. It don't make that much
difference.'

75

CHAPTER 8

The return journey with Troxel as her watchdog left Anne no opportunity to pick up Carmody's trail as she had hoped. When they reached the creek running past her place she drew rein and thanked the Anvil foreman with cool politeness and watched him turn and ride back the way they had come. For a minute she debated waiting until he was out of sight and doubling back to look for Carmody's trail. But a glance at the stars told her it was past midnight now and she felt the weariness of the long day envelop her body and mind and decided against it.

She unsaddled the bay and went toward the glow of lamplight from the house. Caleb was asleep in the kitchen. A Sharp's .50 leaned against the wall at his elbow and the pup was asleep on his lap.

Anne made a noise and he stirred, reaching for the rifle until he saw who it was. Then he said apologetically, 'Must've dozed off.' He glanced at the clock on the wall. 'Good Lord, it's gone past midnight! Where've you been, girl?'

'Anson's,' Anne said wearily as she hung her hat on the antelope rack and took two cups from the shelf, filling them from the coffeepot at the back of the stove.

'Anson's! I thought you went to look for Jeff Carmody.'

'I did. His trail led me there.' She handed him a cup and took one herself and sat down. He waited, watching while she sipped the hot coffee. Then she told him what had happened; how she had trailed Carmody through the fence into Anvil territory, the blood on the ground beneath the junipers at the rim of the valley, and finally about Anson's disturbing story of Carmody's desire for revenge.

There was a long silence when she had finished. At last she looked up and saw Caleb staring thoughtfully at the stove. 'What do you make of it?' she asked.

Caleb shook his head. 'Danged if I know what to make of it, Anne. There's somethin' about it sounds awful fishy – Anson's turnin' friendly all of a sudden is enough to make me suspicious, and yet. . . .' He looked at her. 'How'd he explain the blood under them junipers – or did you ask him?'

'Well – I didn't ask him, but he told me they'd found Creekmore dead on the trail and that Carmody must have killed him when he rode off in a temper. And then when I said that probably explained the blood I'd seen under the junipers Anson looked kind of surprised. Come to think of it, he didn't bother to mention Creekmore until he slipped up and introduced Troxel as his new foreman.'

'What do you make of that?'

'I don't know – unless he was trying to cover up something. It's funny about that blood. There wasn't anything to indicate a man had been shot, you know, no mess on the ground where a body might have lain. The blood looked like it had dripped there, like when you hang a deer carcass over a horse. And there had been two horses there. It doesn't seem likely that Carmody would have shot Creekmore as he was leaving and then bothered to load his body on a horse and sit under those junipers and smoke a cigarette like the signs showed.'

Caleb's eyebrows went up. 'You think it might not have been Creekmore's corpse across that horse?'

Anne stood up, nodding quickly and turning away.

'You think it might have been Jeff?'

Anne sighed. 'I don't know, Caleb. I can't figure it out.' She

77

turned around and said slowly, 'I think I'll ride into town in the morning and have a talk with Mose Dalmas.'

Caleb snorted. 'Might as well save yourself the trouble for all the help you'll get from him.'

'Maybe so. But it isn't just a matter of getting help for myself.'

'You're thinking about Carmody?'

'Yes.'

'But supposin' Anson's told the truth. Supposin' Jeff did kill Creekmore?'

Anne pressed her lips together. 'Then it will mean that everything else Anson said was true – and that will mean I'll need Dalmas to go after Jeff Carmody.'

She turned and started for the door to the bedroom when Caleb stopped her. 'You really believe what Anson said about Jeff?'

'I don't know what to believe, Caleb,' she said wearily. 'I honestly don't know.' She said goodnight and went into the bedroom and closed the door. Caleb stood staring at the door for a long time, then he picked up the Sharps and blew out the lamp and went thoughtfully out of the kitchen toward the bunkhouse.

Despite her weariness Anne did not fall asleep immediately. Doubts and confused thoughts marched through her mind as through an endless maze, seeking outlet. But they found none.

Only one thing stood out clearly now. She loved Jeff Carmody. Loved him for what he had meant to her life in the brief forty-eight hours he had been with her. Loved him for what might have been if things had been different. But now she knew that she faced the pain of disillusion, that her love for him might be love for a man who existed only in her imagination. For if Anson spoke the truth, then there could be no love but only hatred – hatred all the more bitter because she had believed in him and been betrayed.

Her eyes came wide open and she sat up in bed to listen, her heart beating rapidly. There was no mistaking it. The dull rumble of many cloven hoofs pounding on the hard-packed earth. Her eyes swept the flat, searching through the cottonwoods and among the scattered sagebrush beyond. Then she saw them. A small herd of cattle, perhaps thirty or forty, leaving a faint cloud of dust in the moonlight as they came down the slope and across the valley floor toward the house. Beside them a rider darted back and forth, guiding the direction of their stampede, urging them on with the loud slapping of his coiled rope against his boots.

The cattle, she knew instinctively, were hers. It was the rider who held her attention. There was something familiar about him, something in the hat he was wearing, the way the brim rolled, the flat-creased crown. A cry that was almost a sob of anguish escaped her lips. 'Jeff!'

Anne tore herself from the window and ran for the door. 'Caleb!' she screamed.

But he had already heard and was stumbling from the door in his undershirt, pulling on his trousers with one hand and carrying the heavy Sharps in the other.

'Caleb – *look*!' She flung an arm in the direction of the creek, but the old man was already leaning the Sharps against a corral post to steady it. The big buffalo gun shook the night with its roar but the high whine of a riccochet told he had missed.

Anne had watched him shoot, her hand at her throat, in that split second not knowing whether she hoped he would hit or miss. Then the rider's hand moved up and down with a definite motion, the gun in his hand glinting in the moonlight. The window of the bunkhouse burst inward with a tinkle of cascading glass and Caleb bolted through the door cursing and yelling at Anne to get under cover while he got more ammunition for the breech-loading Sharps.

79

The rider's gun exploded again and she saw the lead steer stumble to its knees to be trampled under by the rushing herd, its neck twisting at an awkward angle in the press of heaving bodies. She heard its clear snap above the rumble of the herd and she gave a cry and ran to the kitchen and reached for the Winchester on the wall. The Sharps boomed out again and she spun to the window and peered out. But the rider was still there, firing into the packed and bawling mass of animals. She saw two more go down and she tore the curtain aside and gathered her nightgown above her knees as she rested the rifle across the sill and took aim. But even as she pulled the trigger she knew she had missed in the tricky shadows that surged in the moonlight.

She levered two shots in quick succession as the rider was turning his horse, saw the man's hat snatched from his head and sent spinning across the flat. The Sharps boomed again but the battle was already over. The hat-shot had dampened the marauder's enthusiasm for rifle fire and he spun his mount and disappeared through the trees.

A few minutes later she heard Caleb's footsteps outside and she stood up quickly, brushing her eyes. 'Anne! You all right, Anne!'

'Yes, I'm all right.' She went to the door. He was standing there with the man's hat in his hand.

'He got five of 'em, Anne,' he said sorrowfully. Then he held the hat out to her and said bitterly, 'I guess there ain't no question about who that belonged to, is there?'

She took the hat, thrusting her finger reflectively through the hole in the crown. 'Just two inches lower,' she said, her face grim. 'What a damn shame I missed!' She flung the hat across the room where it bounced off the wall and rolled under the table.

'I can't figure it out,' Caleb said with a slow shake of his head. 'I just can't figure it out. Why would he want to do a thing like that?'

'Why?' Anne said angrily. 'Because he's a killer, that's why! He's come back to get his revenge for spending eight years in prison. Though God knows why he should want to take it out on me. Haven't I suffered enough at his hand? Wasn't it enough for him that I had to lose my husband?'

'But that's just it,' Caleb said insistently. 'He *didn't* kill Clint. And it just don't make sense that he'd have it in for you just because he got sent to prison for a crime he didn't commit. You didn't send him there. The jury did. If he was out for revenge it looks to me like. . . .'

Anne was looking at him strangely. 'You still say he didn't kill Clint, after what happened tonight?' Her voice was quiet, puzzled. She half-lifted her hand to point at him. 'You know something I don't, Caleb. Why do you keep insisting Carmody didn't kill him? Unless' – she took a step toward him as though in a trance, her finger still raised – '*unless you know who did kill him!*'

'Now, Anne, for God's sake, I. . . .'

'What happened while I was back East, Caleb? Did Clint have a run-in with Anson?'

'No, Anne. Anson didn't have nothin' to do with it. I just. . . .'

'Anson killed him, didn't he?' she said, her voice strangely calm, her face composed. 'Anson killed him and because you were afraid of what Anson's men might do to you if you testified against him you lied and said you'd seen him in Canadian the night Clint was shot. Isn't that the way it happened, Caleb – because you were afraid one of Anson's men might kill you if you told the truth?'

'I ain't afraid of Anson! I did see him that night and. . . .'

She leaned toward him suddenly, gripping the edge of the table, her eyes blazing. 'Then why do you keep insisting Carmody is innocent! Do you expect me to believe it after what I saw tonight with my own eyes? Do you? *Do you?*'

He stared at her for a minute, half-afraid she might be

81

going out of her mind. Then he dropped his eyes and heaved a sigh. 'No, Anne,' he said quietly. 'I guess I don't. I just don't think he killed him, that's all. About this other business tonight – well, I just can't figure it out. No matter how hard I try I can't figure it out.'

Anne turned slowly away and walked across the kitchen. When she got to the door she turned, pressing her hand hard against her forehead. 'I'm sorry for what I said, Caleb. I-I don't know what's got into me lately. But I'm tired of trying to figure things out. I'll go see Mose Dalmas in the morning and tell him what happened. I know he's not much of a lawman, but he can't afford to ignore what's happened here tonight.'

She turned to look at him and smiled. 'It's a pity we didn't shoot straighter. Our problem would all be over if we had.' She went inside and closed the door.

Caleb stood staring at the closed door for a long time. 'She tried hard enough,' he murmured. 'Another two inches lower and she'd have killed him. It's pretty hard, Anne, killin' somebody you love. But sometimes it's easier than havin' to hate them if they're alive.' He turned and picked up his Sharps and went out the door and across the yard to the bunkhouse.

Anne slept little during the remainder of the night and she was up at first light, dressed and started the breakfast. When she had made the biscuits and put them in the oven she found she had no eggs. Calling to Caleb as she crossed the yard she went into the henhouse, puzzled at finding the door still open until she remembered that she had ridden off at dusk the night before and neither she nor Caleb had remembered to close it after that.

The hens stirred from their sleep and began clucking as she groped her way among the nests. Her foot struck something and she prodded it with the toe of her boot, then bent swiftly down with a low cry. It was one of her hens, its neck broken and bloody. She struck a match and found another. A black trail of blood leading out the door told her that the coyote, after having his fun, had carried the third hen off for his own breakfast.

She took the eggs and left, crossing the yard just as Caleb came out of the bunkhouse. 'We won't be in business much longer if we keep losing our stock at this rate,' she said.

'Not more dead beef?' Caleb said quickly.

'No, but it's almost easier to replace a steer in this country than a hen. A coyote got in the henhouse last night. I forgot to shut the door. If you have time today you might try to pick up his trail. That's seven he's had this summer.'

They went into the kitchen and Caleb sat at the table while she went back to the stove. 'I'll salt away as much of that beef as I can today,' Caleb said wearily. 'Looks like we'll have enough to last out a siege.'

Caleb stretched his legs under the table to dig in his pocket for his pipe. Feeling something under his foot he bent down and saw it was Carmody's hat still lying there where Anne had thrown it. He picked it up and a folded strip of paper fell out of the sweatband. 'That's funny,' he said, looking at the paper. He found another strip under the sweatband and pulled it out.

'What's funny?' Anne said from the stove.

'This paper in Carmody's hat. The hat's new; I reckon he bought it when he got out of Huntsville. It don't seem likely he'd buy a new hat that didn't fit.'

Anne turned around, frowning. 'What on earth are you muttering about, Caleb? What makes you think it didn't fit?'

He waved a strip of the paper padding. 'This. The sweatband was stuffed with paper because the hat was too big.' Curiously, he unfolded a strip. Then he sat up straight with a cry. 'Anne, come here! Look at this!'

She moved the frying pan to the back of the stove and came over, wiping her hands on her apron. Caleb laid the piece of paper on the table and she picked it up. 'It looks like an order

83

blank out of a mail order catalogue.'

'Yeah – and somebody started to fill it in. Read it.'

'Good Lord!' Anne breathed. 'Allan Vicker, Anvil Ranch, Sand Valley, Texas!' She looked at Caleb, realisation of the meaning leaving a stunned look on her face.

Caleb grinned triumphantly. 'I was right. I said I couldn't figure why Jeff would do a thing like that. It wasn't Jeff. It was Vicker, wearin' Jeff's hat, maybe wearin' the rest of his clothes, too.'

But Anne's face was grim. 'You know what this means, Caleb. I was right about Anson – he lied about Jeff. Lied to cover up. Oh, Caleb, I'm afraid something awful's happened. That blood I saw under the junipers. . . .'

'There now, gal,' Caleb said gently. 'Don't cross your bridges 'fore you come to 'em. Maybe he's only wounded and Anson's got him hid somewhere. Now set down and have your breakfast and when we've finished I'll ride in to town and get hold of Mose. It's time he begun to earn his pay from the county.'

'No – I'd rather go myself,' Anne said. 'It'll give me something to do; something to occupy my mind.'

CHAPTER 9

But the ride to Sand Valley did not take Anne's thoughts off Jeff Carmody. On the contrary, as the dusty miles rolled beneath the fast-moving hoofs of her bay she found her thoughts alternating between hope and dread. Hope that Caleb was right, that Anson had only wounded Carmody and was holding him someplace out of sight, intending to use him as the scapegoat for the attack on Anne's cattle. The dread was the thought that her worst fears might be right, that Carmody might already be dead. She tried to put this thought out of her mind but it kept coming back with agonizing persistence.

When she reached the place on the stage trail where Clint Merriweather's body had been found she reined in and sat for a long time staring at the grassy spot beside the rutted track. Eight years had passed since her life had been shattered by what had happened here. Eight difficult and lonely years, filled with unhappiness and hardships. She found no strangeness in the realization that she thought of Clint almost impersonally now. She had loved him, yes; and she loved him in memory still. But the passage of time had dimmed her recollection of the man who really was, the man who had been her husband but a short eighteen months. She did find it strange that as she gazed at the spot where her husband had died her thoughts were of Jeff Carmody. Perhaps it was because what had happened here had drawn him into her life in an unexpected way; perhaps it was because she found a similarity between them. Or maybe it was because her mind was still clouded with doubt as to what had actually happened in this spot that night eight years ago.

She raised her eyes from beside the trail and gazed out across the sweep of plains, the hot and dusty reaches of the high Panhandle that seemed to stretch on endlessly. This was a hard and violent land, she thought, with little tenderness in it. Women seemed to have no place in it, and yet without the women who stood beside the men there would be no land as she saw it now. The men laboured hard in the hot sun and angry dust to make a living for themselves and their women, yet it seemed that in spite of it all it was the women who suffered most when all things were considered. It was more in a man's nature to face, ungrumbling, the hardships that this land seemed to bring. The violence, the lawlessness; they were part of a man's world, made by men. Yet it was the women who suffered. In eight years she had twice known love, known hope for the future of this country – only to have it torn from her hands and dashed to bitter fragments.

Last night she had tried desperately to kill Jeff Carmody. She shuddered now as she thought of it, and yet it had seemed the far better thing to do than to let the torture of an illusion live on in treachery. Now she had a faint hope that he might still be alive.

The hot wind whipped a whirling column of angry dust along the trail and she closed her eyes against it and moved her horse, spurring him in the direction of town.

It was barely mid-morning when she rode into Sand Valley and got down from her mount in front of Dalmas's office. Opening her saddle-bag she took out Carmody's hat and the folded paper and stepped up to the door. A glance inside told her Dalmas was not around. She went back on the boardwalk and looked up the street and saw him standing under the awning of Gabe Ranson's store talking to a man in rancher's garb. She walked toward them and when she got near she recognized the rancher as Will Henstridge who had given Carmody the pup.

Both men looked up when she approached and touched their hats. Henstridge smiled, but Anne noticed a frown of annoyance flit across Dalmas's face.

'Mornin', Anne,' Will Henstridge said. 'How's the pup gettin' along?'

'Fine, Will. It was good of you to let Penelope have him. She was heartbroken over what happened to the other.'

'Shucks, it wasn't nothin' I did. I'd just have had to drown the little feller, much as I hate that kind of thing. Get too many dogs around the place and they start botherin' the livestock. The man who deserves any credit that's comin' is the feller who rode all that way to fetch the pup. Seemed a likeable gent. Connelly, wasn't that his name?'

Dalmas gave a snort. 'Connelly, hell. I didn't let that name fool me for long. Thought I recognized him when I saw him, but I wasn't sure where. Then I got to thinkin' and dug back in my records. His name's Carmody.'

Henstridge glanced at Anne, then looked away in quick embarrassment. 'You don't mean. . . ?' he said, looking at the sheriff.

Dalmas nodded importantly. 'Same one. He'd still be workin' for Anne if I hadn't put her wise that he was the man who'd shot Clint.'

'That's where you're wrong, Sheriff,' Anne said evenly.

The lawman looked at her queerly. 'Wrong? No, by heck, I ain't wrong. He's changed a little in eight years, but it's the same Carmody or my name ain't. . . .'

'I didn't say he wasn't Carmody,' Anne put in quietly. 'I mean you're wrong about him killing my husband.'

Dalmas shoved back his hat and stared at her in amazement. Then he turned to Henstridge. 'Will, you was at the trial. What did you think?' His tone indicated that he expected immediate agreement. But the rancher dug his thumbs deeper in his gunbelt and stared hard at the boards.

'Since you ask me, Mose,' he said slowly, looking up to meet the sheriff's quizzical gaze, 'I never was quite set in my mind that he'd done it.' When Dalmas flushed angrily he hurried on, 'Oh I know I ain't talkin' *legal* sense – the jury decided he'd done it and that was that. But there was some things about it just didn't fit. Now, you take for one thing. . . .'

She turned to Dalmas. 'I came to see you. Last night a rider herded about fifty of my steers down in front of my house and shot five of them. I managed to shoot his hat off his head before he got away. Here it is. Do you recognize it?'

Henstridge glanced at the hat and blurted, 'Why – that looks like the one. . . .' Then he checked himself, glancing swiftly at Anne.

Dalmas looked up at him, smiling grimly. 'Go ahead, Will. Say it. It looks like the one Carmody was wearin'.'

'I could be wrong,' Henstridge muttered.

'No, Will,' Anne put in. 'You're not wrong. It is Carmody's hat.'

The sheriff stood turning the hat over in his hand. 'Well, it looks plain enough to me, Anne. You fired him when you found out who he was. He was burned up about it, decided he'd get even, came back and shot up your steers. I reckon he's probably left the country by now, but if you want me to have a look for him. . . .' He handed the hat back, his words and manner signifying he didn't think she would want him to. 'But what puzzles me is why he ever came back here in the first place – unless he had some wild notion about taking revenge on you because you was Clint's wife.'

'He came back to find the man who killed Clint,' Anne told him evenly. 'But whether you believe that or not, I want you to find him. And I can tell you where to look.'

Dalmas raised his eyebrows. 'Where?'

'Take a look at this.' Anne handed the paper to him, unfolding it. 'This was stuffed inside the hat. Under the sweatband to make it fit.'

The sheriff read the order blank, then frowned at her. 'I ain't very good at riddles,' he said irritably. 'What's this supposed to mean, if anythin'?'

'That the man who shot my steers last night was Allan Vicker, wearing Carmody's hat. I thought there was something funny going on when I stopped to see Booth Anson and he told me. . . .' She went on to describe her visit to the Anvil ranch in detail, laying emphasis on Anson's sudden attempt to be friendly while relaying Carmody's alleged threats against her. And she finished by mentioning the blood under the junipers and her fears as to what it might indicate.

When she stopped speaking Dalmas smiled as a man might smile at a child who had told an imaginative tale. 'Now hold on, Anne – that's askin' me to believe an awful lot. You ain't got a lot to go on except guesswork, and I think you're just lettin' yourself get excited. I thought you'd be glad Anson finally showed some signs of gettin' friendly. Lord knows you've complained enough about him actin' the other way.'

'Anson actin' friendly toward *anybody* would be enough to make me suspicious,' Will Henstridge said.

The sheriff ignored the remark and pointed to the hat. 'Anne, you say Vicker took this from Carmody and wore it last night. What's to prove it?'

'Why – that mail order blank, of course.'

'And what would keep Carmody from takin' a pencil and fillin' out an old mail order blank and puttin' it under his sweatband to throw suspicion somewhere else in case he lost his hat?'

'Because – because that would be silly!' She realized the remark was inane as soon as she said it, and the lawman's smile made her angry at herself as well as him. 'Well, it would!' she added stubbornly.

Dalmas laughed and handed the hat back to her, saying, 'If you want me to help you, Anne, you'd better offer better proof than female intuition. As a lawman I've got to deal in facts, not guesses. I can't go traipsin' around the county on a wild goose chase just because you *think* somethin's wrong.'

'But Carmody might. . . !'

'Carmody's another matter. If you want to swear out a warrant against him for shootin' your cattle, then I'll do my best to find him for you.'

Anne bit her lip, holding back angry tears. And the knowledge that she was about to cry made her angrier still. Already Dalmas was looking at her with the patient expression of a man who knows he will have a woman's tears to deal with. She glanced quickly at Will Henstridge. The rancher's expression was sympathetic, but she realized he could do nothing and it increased her feeling of helplessness.

She swung her gaze on Dalmas. 'All right! Get your warrant. Only make it out for Allan Vicker!'

Dalmas's smile evaporated and was replaced by a look of consternation. 'Why – I can't arrest Vicker on hearsay evidence, Anne,' he hedged. 'I got to have proof.'

She shook the hat and the piece of paper in his face and said angrily, 'Proof? Here's your proof!'

The sheriff shook his head. 'I'm afraid it ain't good enough to stand up in a court of law.'

Will Henstridge said firmly, 'Maybe you'd better leave that up to judge and jury, Mose. Anne wants you to swear out a warrant. You ain't got no choice.'

Dalmas looked uncomfortable. With a faint smile he said pleadingly, 'Aw, now, Will, I think you're lettin' a woman's tears. . . .'

'And I'm thinkin' you're afraid to set foot on Anvil with a warrant!' the rancher said angrily. 'I didn't figure I'd have to bring this up, Mose, but folks in this county are gettin' just a little fed up at the way you have been pussyfootin' around them Anvil roughnecks lately. Folks are still wonderin' what ever become of Myers and Stalton and' – he turned to Anne – 'what was the names of them other two little outfits just east of Anson's?'

'You mean Sands and Brewer?'

'Yeah, Sands and Brewer.' He faced the sheriff again. 'Anson has taken over quite a bit of territory in the past ten years. And the way he done it don't smell just right to everybody. What's more, he's still pushin'. He's pushin' Anne, here, and you damn well know it! The only reason she ain't gone the same way as Sands and Brewer and the rest of 'em is that maybe even Anson balks at killin' a woman. But that ain't to mention what might have been the cause of Clint Merriweather's death. The point is, Dalmas, it's beginnin' to look like you're scared stiff of Booth Anson. There's talk of formin' a Cattleman's Association here in the county – matter of fact, that's what I'm doin' in town today, if you want to know it. Now if you ain't got guts enough to act like a sheriff, then by God come election this fall the association'll put somebody in your place who has.'

Fifteen minutes later Anne came out of the sheriff's office followed by Dalmas. The lawman's face was ashen beneath his deep tan. He touched his hat to her and said a curt good morning and strode across the street toward the livery stable, his lips pressed grimly together. A white piece of paper protruded from his shirt pocket and he fingered it uneasily as he turned in at Buckley's shouting for the man to saddle his horse.

Anne watched him go and felt a little sorry for him. Then she turned and walked into Ranson's store to buy a sack of coffee she'd forgotten on her last trip. Gabe Ranson was handing it to her when he said suddenly, 'Say, I just remembered somethin'. That young feller who went to work for you was askin' about a pair of spurs the other day. I forgot exactly whether he wanted to know but you can tell him I can get 'em for him if he still wants 'em. I happen to run across an old catalogue with 'em in yesterday and found I'd ordered the same kind for Caleb a few years back. But you tell him, will you?'

'All right, I'll tell him,' Anne said absently.

CHAPTER 10

It was still night when Carmody wakened but the shaft of moonlight through the window had shifted to the east wall and told him the moon was low in the west. He judged it was close to morning and lay awake for a while, wondering what had wakened him.

Some of the pain had gone out of his chest and now there was only a bruised feeling and a slight burning sensation along the length of the wound. He was pleasantly surprised to find that the sleep had left him feeling much stronger and wondered if he might have underestimated his recuperative powers.

With deliberate slowness he swung his feet to the floor and sat, head bowed, on the edge of the bed until the giddiness had passed. Then he got to his feet and, still moving slowly on unsteady legs, crossed to the window and peered out. It was then that he saw what had awakened him.

A rider was unsaddling by moonlight down at the corral and when he had finished he crawled through the bars and came at a fast walk toward the house. It was Vicker, Carmody realized, and he noticed that the man was hatless. Drawing back into the shadow of the window as the rider came up the walk, Carmody watched him slow his approach and step cautiously up to the veranda.

'Booth!' the man called quietly. 'Booth – it's me, Vicker!'

There was a sound of movement as if someone had been awakened from sleep and a pair of boots thudded to the floor.

'Vicker, that you? Come on in. I fell asleep on this damn couch waitin' for you to come back. What happened; everythin' go all right?'

Vicker was out of sight now beneath the roof of the veranda, but Carmody heard him cross to the window to talk to the man inside. 'By God I ain't gonna try *that* again! I choused about forty head of their stock right up in front of the house and started to pistol 'em when the old man cut loose with a damn buffalo gun and like to scared the spit out of me. Then the gal opened up with a Winchester from the house and her third and fourth shot took the hat clean off my head – just like somebody'd reached up and grabbed it. Hell, an inch lower and she'd've had me!'

'Aw, quit your bellyachin',' Anson growled. 'You make it sound like you'd been in a gunfight instead of tryin' to scare an old man and a woman. Did you kill any of their beef?'

'Yeah, I got five. But by damn they like to got me, too. The next time. . . .'

'Did you get close enough for them to see who you was supposed to be, that's what I want to know?'

'Hell, yes. And anyway they ain't gonna have any doubt about who it was when they find Carmody's hat there in the mornin'.'

Anson chuckled appreciatively. 'No, they sure ain't. Well, we'll hit 'em again tomorrow night and maybe the next. By that time they ought to be ready to believe Carmody's got it in for them. Well, you had a pretty good night – you better sleep in in the morning'.'

'Thanks,' Vicker mumbled sarcastically as he left the porch.

Carmody stood for a while digesting what he had heard, frowning. Anne had lost five steers she could ill afford; and this had been but a token raid. But that was relatively unimportant. What worried him most was her helplessness; she and Caleb alone trying to stand up to Anson. Then he smiled grimly. From Vicker's account they had made a pretty good showing for themselves. Yet no matter how valiantly they fought they could

93

never expect to hold the place against twenty armed men when the showdown came. The house would be a flaming death trap once it caught fire. He realized he could not wait the full five days he had counted on. As soon as he could drag himself into a saddle he would have to leave to warn them. Not only to warn them, but also the very fact of his leaving would spoil Anson's plan. It would leave him without a dead Carmody to dump behind to be blamed for what had happened.

He heard Anson's footsteps on the stairs and realized the man was coming up to bed. Moving on unsteady legs he managed to regain his bed just as the lamplight loomed bright on the stairs. He lay back and closed his eyes, feigning sleep. Anson came to the top of the stairs and halted, peering into the room. Carmody could tell he was there, could hear him breathing, could see the brightness of the lamp through his eyelids. Presently Anson moved away down the hall and he heard him place the lamp on something solid in another room and opened his eyes.

The light from the other room threw Anson's shadow large in the hall. The man undressed; Carmody watching the shadow saw him take off his gunbelt and heard the clank of steel-loaded leather as the man hung it on the iron bedstead. In a few minutes a heavy snore drifted through the upper rooms.

Carmody lay awake for a while longer, thinking. Evidently Anson considered Carmody sufficiently disabled to dispense with a guard. This aroused a burning temptation as Carmody speculated his chances of leaving while the man slept. He raised himself up and glanced through the door, his heartbeat quickening at the thought. The snores grew into a measured rhythm as Anson relaxed into deep sleep.

Carmody shook his head despairingly and sank back on the bed. Even if Anson did not waken, he doubted if he had sufficient strength to make his way down the stairs, across the yard to the corral, saddle a horse and get away. Not yet. In another night or two, maybe. But not yet.

When he awoke again it was full daylight and someone was shaking him gently. He opened his eyes to find an elderly negro standing beside the bed watching him with large brown eyes and proffering a plate of food. 'You feel strong enough to eat sumpin', suh?' he asked gently in a rich, deep voice.

Carmody started to say automatically that he felt strong enough to eat a horse, then checked himself.

I-I think so,' he said feebly. 'Can you help me to sit up – I'm still pretty weak.'

The man nodded in a kindly way and put the plate on the chair, then he came back and helped Carmody to sit up, his hands as careful and gentle as a woman's. 'You sho' lost a pow'ful lot of blood, suh,' he said, handing Carmody the plate.

The negro made no sign of leaving but stood patiently waiting for Carmody to finish, the large eyes following each mouthful of food to its destination with obvious solicitude. Carmody forced himself to eat slowly, giving the impression of toying with his food.

He was surprised at how well he had slept, how well he felt. His chest still pained him and the bruised feeling seemed to have spread around his whole rib cage, leaving him stiff and sore when he moved the fork to his mouth. But the pain itself was nothing; it was his strength that was important and he was overjoyed to see that it was fast returning.

He turned to the negro, speaking slowly to continue the impression of weakness. 'How long have you worked for Anson?'

The man glanced at the door uneasily then wagged his grizzled head. 'Too long, suh,' he said, with a faint smile.

Carmody continued eating thoughtfully. The old man was obviously the cook and general flunky, but there was something odd about his being here. There was too much refinement about him for a common ranch cook, too much of an air of gentility. 'You don't come from this part of the country,' Carmody said.

'No, suh. Ah's from Vicksburg, Mississippi.'

'You don't like Texas?'

The old man grinned apologetically. 'Beggin' yo' pardon, suh – kase you a Texan – no suh. Ah'd lak t' be back whar I kin see the old rivuh at sunset.' He sighed and stared into the distance. 'But hit doan lok lake Wash evuh goan back.'

Carmody looked up from his plate. 'Why not?'

'Mistuh Booth – he woan let me.'

'Won't let you? Hell, he don't own you.'

'He say he do. Mistuh Booth say he kill me if'n Ah try to run away. An' Ah know he'd do it, too.'

Carmody was turning the thing swiftly in his mind while Wash was speaking. There was a chance that Wash might have been sent here by Anson to sound him out, but it was a slim chance. The old man's story sounded genuine enough and it tallied with his opinion of Anson. He said suddenly, 'Wash, can you saddle a horse?'

Wash looked at him a moment, suspiciously, his eyes moving uneasily to the door and back again. 'What you schemin' to do suh? They's watchin' me all the time. Ah's afraid to try. . .'

'Not you, Wash. Me,' Carmody said, keeping his voice low.

'You, suh? You ain' in no fitten shape to ride no. . . .'

'Look,' Carmody said. He swung his legs out of bed and stood up. Giddiness seized him and he tottered for a minute. Then it passed and he grinned at the old negro staring goggle-eyed. 'I'm still a little weak, but I've been playin' possum. I'm not as bad as I've let them think, because as soon as I look well enough you know what Anson aims to do.'

Wash nodded and Carmody went on. 'I'm strong enough to ride once I get in the saddle, but' – he lifted his arms slowly, wincing at the pain in his chest – 'I don't think I could manage to lift a saddle for a day or two. And by that time it might be too late. Now, if you could saddle one for me. . . .'

Wash stared at the plate he was holding and Carmody noticed the hands were shaking with emotion. Slowly the old eyes raised to meet his own. 'Ah'll do it, suh. Fo' you an' Missus

Merriweather an' her chile – ah'll git yo' a hoss.'

Carmody clapped him on the shoulder and said earnestly, 'Wash, how'd you like to go back to Mississipi?'

'Miss. . . ?' The old man's voice broke, his eyes lighting with hope. 'Lawdy, suh – you aint joshing po' ole Wash is you?'

Carmody shook his head. 'No, Wash, I ain't joshin'.'

'B-but Mistuh Booth . . . he woan let me. . . .'

'Mister Booth ain't gonna be around to stop you. When this is all over I'm buyin' you a railroad ticket to Vicksburg.'

Tears welled up in the old eyes and Wash raised a finger to brush them away, shaking his head. 'Vicksburg!' he murmured. 'Ah din' think Ah'd ebber cross dat ole ribber again. Ah-Ah just cain't believe it!'

Carmody crossed to the window and peered cautiously out to see that no one was below who might happen to look up. Then he swept the sprawling outbuildings with his gaze and called, 'Wash, come here. See that clump of live oak just beyond the corral?'

'Yassuh.'

'All right, here's what I want you to do. Sometime between dusk and moonrise tonight you saddle a horse and tie him in that clump. And be sure you tie him with a rope, not the reins. I don't want him to spook and slip his bridle if there's any shootin'.'

'Shootin'? Lawd, I hope they's no shootin', suh – an' you wifout no gun.'

'Plenty of guns downstairs in Anson's study when the time comes,' Carmody said, leaving the window. 'What time do they generally eat supper?'

'Long 'bout dusk.'

'So it'll be dark when they finish.'

Wash mused. 'Purty dahk. Some eats quicker'n others.'

'Does Anson eat with his crew?'

'Most times – when he ain't got visitors.'

'You have to be there?'

'Yassuh. Ah waits the table.'

Carmody frowned. 'That ain't so good. I'd counted on you slipping away while they ate. But if you've got to be there it won't give you time to get that horse staked out.'

'Ah'll manage, suh. They usually sits around talkin' or playin' cards when they's finished supper.'

Wash scurried down the stairs and Carmody heard him muttering as he passed Anson, 'Yassuh, that gen'lmun up yonder he's so weak he couldn't feed hisse'f an' Ah had to spoon hit for him.'

Carmody, back in bed now, grinned at Wash's lie and blessed him for his quick thinking. Anson said, 'Still weak, huh? I'd better take a look.' He lumbered up the stairs and into the room, eying Carmody speculatively from the doorway. Carmody turned listlessly on the bed and stared at him.

'Feelin' any better?' Anson asked belligerently.

'A little,' Carmody replied feebly.'

Anson shrugged. 'Well, it don't make a damn to me. If you ain't well enough to ride tomorrow night we'll tie you across a saddle and haul you there. You ain't gonna live long anyhow, so what's the use pamperin' you?'

'I'll live to see you in hell,' Carmody said quietly.

The Anson owner grinned slyly. 'Y'know something, Carmody? I don't think you're as feeble as you let on. You might've fooled that nigger cook of mine, but you ain't foolin' me. I seen the plate of vittles he carried over here, and that plate was plumb clean as a licked cat when he took it past me now. Any man can eat that good ain't feelin' too bad. Maybe you did lose a lot of blood, but you got enough spit and vinegar left in you to make up for a barrel of blood. It might give you ideas about leavin' before I'm ready for you to.'

Carmody's smile faded when Anson had gone and he frowned. He might have figured Anson was too slick to be easily fooled. Now he guessed he'd have a guard put on him. He didn't like that. He didn't like that at all.

98

CHAPTER 11

Carmody heard a door slam and the thud of Anson's boots leaving the verandah. He sat up in bed and looked out the window to see Anson crossing the wagon yard toward the bunkhouse. A few minutes later a rider came out with Anson and they stood talking for a while, then the rider nodded and started for the house. Carmody lay back and presently he heard the man coming up the stairs.

When the newcomer stood in the doorway and glanced at the captive, Carmody felt a ray of hope. He had expected Anson to send an older hand, possibly Vicker or Troxel. But this fellow was a kid who had not yet seen his twentieth year. If it came to a test of strength, even in his weakened condition Carmody felt he had more than an even chance. Then he glanced at the kid's face and his confidence waned.

It was the eyes that made the difference. Pale, colourless eyes. The eyes – and the long, tapering fingers caressing the smooth cedar grips of the holstered .45. Right then Carmody knew he would welcome Vicker or Troxel in exchange for this youngster. An older man would have a natural caution that came with experience. This kid had not lived long enough to have learned that a little fear is sometimes a good thing. And that made him doubly dangerous.

The pale eyes passed over Carmody without a flicker of personal interest in the man they saw, they only weighed him

99

up as a possible target if it came to trouble. Then the kid hooked the chair toward him with his toe and tilted back against the wall to roll a cigarette.

Carmody moved his hand to scratch his head. He made the movement deliberately sudden so that it might be interpreted as an aggressive one.

There was no sudden start, no scuffling of feet or frantic tugging at the holstered gun. There was only a vague impression of movement. One minute the kid had been staring out the window; the next instant Carmody found himself pinned by three things; a pair of cold eyes and the colder eye of the .45.

The kid's voice when he spoke was surprisingly deep and unhurried. 'Don't make no fast move like that again or I'll kill you,' he drawled. There was no anger in the words, they hardly sounded more than a simple statement. But they made a brief chill course down Carmody's spine despite the gathering heat of the mid-morning sun. The gun slid away and the kid returned his gaze to the window as though nothing had happened.

Carmody tried a question. 'You ever use that gun on a man, son?' he said quietly.

The eyes moved to him. 'Don't "son" me,' the voice said flatly. And this time the eyes had changed slightly, showing just a flicker of anger. Carmody lay back, staring at the ceiling. But inwardly he was smiling. He had found a crack in the armour. The kid was touchy about his lack of years.

Carmody guessed the reason. Here was a youngster who had practised with a gun until he had mastered it. Every move he made with it would be as flawless as that lightning-like, fluidly effortless draw Carmody had just witnessed. He was good, and he knew it. No man could beat him – with a gun. And he had probably put his meagre intelligence to work and figured that if he hired out that gun he could make himself a reputation and a pile of money. Only he had found that in the world of men he was tolerated only because of his gun, but tolerated smilingly because of his lack of stature in years. And that, Carmody saw plainly, rankled him.

It was high noon when Wash wakened him, standing there beside the bed with a plate in his hand. The kid was still there, eating mechanically from a plate on the washstand beside him. He did not bother to look at Carmody, but Carmody knew he was watching.

Wash made a show of helping Carmody to sit up and said pointedly, 'I cut hit up fo' you, suh, so's you could manage hit.'

Wash left this time before waiting for them to finish eating. The kid left his plate on the washstand and returned his chair to its tilted position against the wall, ignoring Carmody's empty plate on the bed. He belched contentedly and rolled a smoke and lit it.

'I could sure use a smoke,' Carmody said pointedly.

'Go right ahead.'

'My tobacco's in my shirt – and Vicker's got that.'

The kid merely shrugged and went on calmly smoking and gazing out of the window again. Hell, Carmody thought, he's cold clean through. Even Vicker let me borrow his makin's. His nostrils quivered at the sweet smell of tobacco and he watched hungrily as the kid dragged smoke deep into his lungs and exhaled. He was on the point of asking outright when he thought to hell with it. Asking Vicker for a smoke had been one thing. But he was damned if he was going to give this gunsmart yearling a chance to turn him down. He ground his teeth and lay back and closed his eyes, thinking, 'All right, buster. Wait till tonight. I'll put some expression into that poker face of yours.'

He gradually let his irritation simmer, and then he dozed. It must have been about fifteen minutes later by his reckoning when he heard a door slam down below and the sound of running boots on the gravel. A voice called, 'Booth! Booth, here comes Mose Dalmas.'

101

He opened his eyes and saw the kid standing beside the window looking out, deadpan as ever. Carmody sat up, slowly, and spoke to let the kid know he was moving. 'The sheriff?' he said quietly. The pale eyes turned. 'Try it,' the kid said ominously. 'Just try it, that's all.'

'Try what – son?' Carmody said deliberately.

The kid whirled, his gun coming out in a blur of movement and Carmody held his breath. But the kid had no intention of shooting with the sheriff within earshot; instead he flipped the gun expertly, caught it by the barrel. Advancing to the side of the bed, his face livid with uncontrollable rage, he drew back the gun as if to strike. 'God damn you!' he breathed between clenched teeth. 'You call me that once more and I'll bust your head wide open with the butt of this pistol!'

Carmody stared at him, stared deep into those angry pale eyes, and smiled a little smile; just enough to tease the kid, to let him know he wasn't afraid. Just piling a little more brush on until it was time to fan the spark into a flame. 'Sonny,' he thought behind the smile, 'you're real handy with that peacemaker. I'll bet you practised hours to get that flip down just right, and it looks real fancy. But – you got a lesson comin', and I'll teach it to you tonight. Don't never swing a gun by the barrel. If you do, somebody's liable to grab the butt end and blow your brains out.'

'Keep back from that window!' the kid hissed.

Carmody glanced at him. 'I won't show myself, s. . . .' He stopped on the sibilant as the kid whirled again, glowering. Carmody smiled and turned to peer over the sill as the slow clop of the sheriff's horse sounded on the hardpan below.

Looking at an angle he could see the front gate and the men beside it. Anson and his foreman, Troxel, and Vicker. The three of them lounged against the fence conversing in low tones. The sheriff came into Carmody's line of vision and Anson called out, 'Howdy, Mose. Light and rest a spell. Hell of a hot day for you to be joy-ridin'.'

Dalmas pulled in but did not dismount. Carmody could see the man was plainly nervous. Then he noticed a square of white paper sticking from his shirt pocket and wondered if that had anything to do with it.

'This ain't no joy-ride, Booth,' Dalmas said uneasily. 'It's a business call.' Then he hurried on apologetically. 'Now I want you to understand there ain't nothin' personal in this, far's I'm concerned. I just got a duty to perform, unpleasant as it is. . . .'

'I'll bet it's unpleasant,' Anson cut in sharply. 'For you. You're shakin' like jelly. All right – let's hear it.'

Dalmas moved his gaze uncomfortably from Anson to Vicker. He touched the paper in his pocket hesitantly and said, 'It's for you, Vicker. I got a warrant for your arrest.'

Vicker and Anson glanced quickly at each other; Vicker's facing showing uncertainty, Anson's openly puzzled. Looking up at Dalmas, Anson said querulously, 'You got *what?*'

'A warrant for Vicker's arrest. It ain't my doin', Booth. I'm just here to serve it. Anne Merriweather made it out and. . . .'

'Oh, so that's it!' Anson snarled. 'You're lettin' her run your office now!'

Dalmas eyed him uncomfortably. 'You know that ain't so, Booth. But I got a job to do and I'm doin' it. But I don't think. . . .'

'Now hold on a minute – what's she got against Vicker?'

'She says he shot down five of her beef last night.'

Vicker blurted, 'Aw, hell, she's crazy! Why I. . . .'

Anson glared him into silence then turned to the lawman. 'Now ain't that just like a woman? I went out of my way yesterday to try and be friendly with her and show I was willin' to bury the hatchet. And this is what I get for it!'

'Well – I know you're doin' your best to be friendly with her, Booth. She told me herself how friendly you'd acted. Only that's just the point, accordin' to her. She's suspicious of you actin' friendly. She claims it's just to cover up for what you're tryin' to do and. . . .'

'Hell, she can't send you out here to arrest one of my men just because she's suspicious! If she's tryin' to pin a serious charge on Anvil she'll need proof, not suspicion.' Anson leaned over the fence, wagging a finger at Dalmas. 'By damn I know who done it – and I told her yesterday he was out to cause trouble. Carmody. That's who. Now you just look at what happened after he. . . .'

'She says it wasn't Carmody. She claims you've got Carmody locked up here – either that or you've killed him and. . . .'

Anson slammed his hand on a fencepost with a resounding thwack. 'By God that's an outrage! She ought'n be allowed to go around accusin' people of anythin' that comes into her head. And I don't give a damn if she is a woman, she. . . .' Anson broke off, calming his fury a little. He jerked open the gate. 'Here. Tell you what you do, Mose. You have a look. Look in the house, the barns, ride all the hell over Anvil range lookin' for a fresh grave if you want. If you think I've got Carmody here, then by damn have a look.'

Upstairs, Carmody's heart skipped a beat. If Dalmas took him up on it the lid would sure blow off. He stole a glance at the kid and saw the kid had his gun out. 'Take it easy, mister!' the kid said tight-lipped. 'If that old fool comes pokin' his nose in here. . . .'

But Dalmas had no stomach for making a search of Anvil. He shook his head quickly. 'Hell, Booth – I know you ain't got him here.'

Anson let the gate close and leaned on it. 'Of course I ain't. Of all the damn silly things I ever heard. What the devil would I want to keep him here for anyway?'

Carmody thought, 'If I tackle the kid now and let out a yell. . . .' then he dismissed the thought. It would be signing Mose Dalmas's death warrant. Anson would never let him live to leave Anvil with that knowledge.

Down below Dalmas was saying, 'Well, that's what I thought.

But anyway, here's this warrant and I'm servin' it. I told her she didn't have enough proof to hold up in court, so I don't reckon it'll come to much.'

'Proof! What kind of proof *has* she got?'

'Well – she found Carmody's hat. . . .'

'Hell! Then go find Carmody.'

'. . . and inside the hat she found a piece of paper – a mail order blank – with Vicker's name on it. Claims Vicker took the hat for a disguise to make her think it was Carmody.'

Anson guffawed. 'Then she can go fiddle. I never heard anythin' so crazy.' But he turned to look at Vicker and even from where he watched Carmody could see the venom in the glance for the man's stupidity.

'I got to serve this warrant, Booth. Crazy or not. It's the law. I tried to argue her out of it, but Will Henstridge was there and he said. . . .'

'Henstridge! What the hell's he got to do with it?'

'Well—' Dalmas began, his uneasiness growing, 'he claimed I was bowin' too much to Anvil and that the cattlemen in the county are gettin' fed up with it and they're formin' some kind of an association to make you pull in your horns. He said if I didn't serve this warrant they'd put in a man at election time of their own choosin'.'

Anson stared, flabbergasted. Then he straightened and shoved back his hat. 'So that's the way it is, is it?'

Dalmas nodded. ' 'Fraid so, Booth. But you know me, I never play favourites.'

'So you're turnin' on me because of this damn association!' Anson roared. 'Afraid to stand up for what's right because they might vote you out from behind that nickleplated star!'

'You know that ain't so, Booth,' Dalmas said, fidgeting in the saddle. He glanced at Vicker. 'You comin'?'

Vicker stepped a little aside from the others. He looked disdainfully up at the man on horseback, his hand brushing his gun. 'You takin' me?' he taunted.

105

Anson shifted his eyes from one to the other quickly, then said, 'Take off your gun, Vicker, you're goin' with Mose.'

Vicker whirled on Anson, demanding angrily, 'What the hell, Booth? I ain't done nothin'.'

'I know you ain't. But the sheriff's got a warrant for you and he's got to serve it. All right, look at it this way. You're in jail for shootin' Merriweather steers. But Carmody ain't gonna know that. Sooner or later he'll come back and try it again. With you in jail there aint' gonna be no doubt about who's really doin' the shootin', is there? See what I mean?' Anson dropped his offside eyelid in a slow wink that was hidden from the sheriff.

Vicker straightened, his hand leaving his gun. 'Why – yeah, I begin to see now. Yeah, that makes sense all right.' He unbuckled his belt and handed it to his boss. 'See you in church,' he grinned. 'All right, Sheriff, I'm comin'. Just let me fetch my horse.'

Dalmas relaxed visibly, shoving his hat back and wiping the sweat from his brow. Then he began an innocuous conversation with Anson about the weather and state of the graze.

Upstairs Carmody was watching the kid's reaction to what had happened. It was beyond the gunsharp's mental ability to grasp the meaning of Anson's move. The whole scene had presented itself to his mind in clear black and white; the sheriff had tried to take away an Anvil man, therefore the sheriff deserved killing.

'What the hell's Booth doin'?' he said in cold fury. 'Why didn't he gun the old fool down? I got a good mind to try it from here myself. By damn I think I will.' He lifted his gun, taking aim through the open window.

'I wouldn't if I was you,' Carmody said quietly, lying back on the bed.

The eyes shifted to his face, half belligerent, half questioning. 'Why the hell not? You think I'm afraid to gun a lawman?'

'No. But Booth'll be madder'n hell if you do. He wants Vicker in jail – didn't you hear what he said?'

The kid's face frowned with the exertion of thought. He glanced out of the window in time to see Vicker and the sheriff ride off. He shook his head. 'Well, it's too late now. I reckon Booth knows what he's doin'. But if it'd been me I'd of gunned him down.'

Carmody sighed and closed his eyes. He didn't particularly like Mose Dalmas, but he would hate to see him killed and not try to stop it. At least he had found out something that changed his opinion of Dalmas. The man wasn't a hired tool of Booth Anson, he was just plain afraid of him. And Carmody could understand that. Fear was a human thing. It didn't make him like Dalmas any more than before, but at least now he felt he understood him better.

His mind did not dwell long on Mose Dalmas. It was Anson's move that worried him now. The man's intentions were all too plain from what he had told Vicker. With Vicker in jail it would be an ideal time to make the big raid on the Merriweather place. Anne had sworn out the warrant over the sheriff's objections, confident in her belief in Vicker's guilt. But after the raid, with Anne and Caleb and Penelope dead, and with Carmody's body dumped along the creek as evidence of what had happened, Mose Dalmas would be only too quick to vindicate himself by pointing out that he had been right in suspecting Carmody all along. And Dalmas could blame Will Henstridge and his unformed cattleman's association for the pressure which had made him arrest Vicker against his better judgment. It would leave Anson in the clear – hadn't he told the sheriff he was making a mistake in arresting Vicker, that Carmody had threatened to do this?

What worried him most was that Vicker's arrest would make Anson itch to get on with the job. He had counted on four days, maybe five, in which to recoup his strength. But time was running out, and running fast. Unless he missed his guess,

Anson would want to strike immediately.

A few minutes later he heard Anson's heavy tread on the stairs and he knew with a sinking heart that he had guessed right. He opened his eyes and saw the Anvil owner standing in the doorway grinning at him.

'You heard what happened out there, I guess?' Anson said.

Carmody nodded. 'Yeah, I heard.'

'Then I guess you know what's goin' to happen to you tonight.'

'From the back, Anson?' Carmody said.

'Not this time, friend. I want to watch the look on your face when you see it comin'.' He turned to the kid called Peabody. 'We'll be eatin' early tonight. I want to hit the Merriweather place just at dark when they'll be havin' supper. I want to be back here before moonrise just in case somebody might be nosin' around who might see us. Keep an eye on him. I got a hunch he ain't as bad sick as he tries to make out, and he might try to slip out.'

The pale eyes switched eagerly to Carmody. 'I'll watch him. And I hope he does try somethin'. That's all the excuse I want.'

'None of that!' Anson said angrily. 'I ain't havin' you steal my fun. Clout him if you have to, or shoot him in the leg or somethin'. But I want him alive, understand!' He looked at Carmody. 'I want him to hear the Merriweather gal scream when we pour coal oil over her and strike a match.'

Carmody jerked upright in bed. 'You dirty. . . !'——

Anson laughed silently. 'Pretty frisky all of a sudden for a sick man, ain't you, Buster?' He turned away and went down the stairs laughing.

CHAPTER 12

A cool breeze moved through the uncurtained window and Carmody realized with a sinking feeling that it was the first cool of approaching evening. The sound of bustling preparation began to be heard down the corrals as mounts were caught and saddled and led to the hitchrack outside the bunkhouse. He heard Anson's voice reminding somebody to make sure the corks were hammered tight into the jugs of coal oil they were taking along.

Footsteps came cautiously up the stairs and Wash appeared in the doorway. The old man glanced uneasily at Peabody, then looked at Carmody. 'They's eatin' early tonight, suh. Ah was wonderin' effin' you wanted to eat wif'em or maybe later.' The question in Wash's eyes was plainer than the question in his words. Did Carmody want to try to get away before the others left; or did he want to let them leave first so that he would have a better chance? Obviously Wash did not know how Anson planned to do it – this killing of Carmody.

The kid spoke up before Carmody could answer. 'Don't worry about him. He won't even need to eat. He won't have time to digest it even. It'd be a waste of food.'

Wash did not turn when the kid spoke. His eyes were on Carmody and they grew wide with fear.

Carmody said, 'I don't want any more horsemeat anyway. If it's dark and you can't see what you're eatin', that's one thing.

But don't you bother about any of that horsemeat for me, understand?'

'Yassuh,' Wash said, 'Ah unnerstan'. But Ah just thought Ah'd come up an' tell you hit's all ready anyway, anytime you wants hit.' He glanced through the window without raising his head for the kid to see. 'Hit's right out dere, dat hossmeat as you calls it – jus' waitin' fo' you.'

'All ready. . . ?' Carmody said, then stopped.

'Yassuh,' Wash said quietly, and as he turned away he smiled triumphantly at the look of surprise in Carmody's eyes.

When Wash had gone Carmody lay back and closed his eyes, but his heart was pounding furiously. Good old Wash! But he'd taken a big chance saddling that horse in broad daylight.

Slowly, as though moving in his sleep, he moved his arms, raising them one at a time above his head to grasp the iron frame of the bedstead, testing the muscles in his chest. There was a little pain now, but only a barely perceptible weakness. He felt a surge of exhilaration.

Relaxing, he opened one eye a slit and looked out of the window at the tops of the trees. About half an hour till sundown. They would all be eating then. That would be the time to do it. Half an hour. Could he lie here that long without moving around, without going crazy waiting?

The sudden clanging of the triangle shattered the evening stillness and seemed to continue an interminable time before it finally stopped. That would be Wash making sure that Carmody heard.

The kid got up and went out the stairway and peered down, glowering. He came back and said, more to himself than Carmody, 'That black devil! He didn't bring me nothin' to eat.' He kicked the chair savagely and sent it spinning, cursing Wash obscenely.

'Maybe he figured you wasn't hungry, son,' Carmody said quietly.

110

The kid whirled, hand whipping downwards to his gun, his face livid. 'Damn you, I said don't call me that!'

He was standing, spraddle-legged, quivering with anger. Carmody took a deep breath to steady his own voice and said, 'Remember what Anson said – he wouldn't be exactly happy if you did what you're thinkin' of doin'.'

'Then don't call me that! He said I could clout you – and I will if you say that again.'

'Why, it just come kind of natural. I always say that to anybody who ain't dry behind the ears yet, son.'

The kid whipped out his pistol, flipped it in that expert way, catching it by the barrel and standing over Carmody. 'Once more!' he hissed between clenched teeth. 'Just call me that once more and I'll pound your brains out!'

'Now don't get excited, son. You. . . .'

That triggered it. Carmody saw the kid draw back and swing down, aiming at his head. He waited, measuring the swing, splitting the fraction of a second it took for the butt to begin its downward arc. Then he changed from a wounded man on a bed into a surprisingly dangerous adversary, and from the startled look in Peabody's eyes he saw that the kid realized too late the mistake he had made.

Carmody's right hand closed over the down-swinging pistol butt and jerked it. The kid tried to hold on, but the smooth barrel gave no grip, the gun came easily into Carmody's hand. In one uninterrupted motion he came off the bed, swinging his left fist as he drew the gun away in his right. The kid was caught off balance at the end of his down-swing, Carmody's fist crashed against the unprotected face, sent the gunsharp flying awkwardly against the wall.

The kid was staggering groggily, his mouth dribbling blood, his fear-laden eyes trying to locate Carmody. Carmody located him first – with the barrel of the .45 just behind the left ear. The kid collapsed like a wet gunnysack and lay in an unmoving heap. 'Never swing a gun by the barrel, kid – I said I'd teach you the right way!'

He moved quickly, bending swiftly and stripping off the kid's outer clothing, boots first, and then gunbelt. The boots were tight and pinched his feet, but it was no time to be choosy. He lifted the inert form onto the bed and began ripping the blanket into strips.

It took several precious minutes to spread-eagle the kid and tie him hand and foot to the bedstead and gag him firmly. But they were minutes well spent. Every second that his departure went unnoticed meant distance between him and Anvil. When he had finished he stepped to the window for a quick look.

All was quiet in the gathering twilight. A dozen mounts stood saddled and waiting. He counted them carefully, filing the information away for future use. His eyes shifted to the clump of live oak beyond the buildings and for a second or two doubt assailed him heavily. He could see no horse from here, but he supposed Wash would have hidden it well.

He fought off the notion. It had to be there. If it wasn't. . . . His eyes moved back to the dozen waiting mounts and he shook his head. There was the faint glow of lamplight from the window where the eating crew now sat. It would be impossible to take a horse from under their noses and live to tell about it. He took a last look at the layout of the buildings, marking his course to the oaks. Then he turned and went swiftly but quietly down the stairs.

In the hall below he thought of the map with the crosses and skulls in the japanned box. Damning evidence which, tied with what he knew now, would end Anson's empire for ever. But time was ticking steadily away and soon the riders would begin to trickle out of the cookshack. Reluctantly he turned from the hall into the kitchen and crossed carefully onto the back porch.

From back here he would be out of sight of anybody in or around the cookshack, shielded by the intervening buildings.

With a hasty glance to assure himself that the yard was clear, he opened the screen door and closed it quietly and began running across the yard. He gained the back of the barn and paused, listening. From around the corner came the low murmur of voices and sounds of eating. He hurried on, leaving the barn and ducking low behind the fence that joined the lesser outbuildings.

There was scattered sagebrush here and he made good use of its cover, running low, dodging deeper and deeper into it, angling away from the buildings. At last he came to the place that had bothered him most – an open stretch of some fifty yards between the nearest sagebrush and the sheltering clump of oak. He slid the gun from its holster and checked the load. He did not reholster it, but held it ready, glancing toward the cookshack, gauging the run across the open. The horses still stood as they were, no sign of movement came yet from the building. But already the sun was gone from the rim of the valley to the west and he knew he had no time to waste.

He ran across the open stretch, half expecting to hear a shout or the whine of a bullet, and pleasantly surprised when he raised nothing more than a startled jackrabbit. Then he found the horse.

He came upon it slowly, talking in low tones to quiet it, running his eyes over the mount. And he blessed Wash. The animal was a black gelding, short-coupled and deep-barreled and built for speed. It looked sleek and well-cared for and was obviously not an ordinary working bronc out of anybody's string. The Anvil brand was plainly etched on the glistening flank and Carmody grinned briefly and wondered how Anson would feel if he knew one of his own personal mounts was to snatch Carmody away from him.

Untying the lead rope Carmody led the black to the edge of the oaks farthest from the buildings and mounted. He raised his head and marked his course through the covering brush as far as he could, then he picked a distant V in the hills to the

113

north-west which he hoped would bring him out near the Merriweather ranch. He did this in one sweeping glance as he mounted, then reined the black when he heard a voice say, 'That'll do, Carmody. Hold it right there!'

There was a movement in the brush directly ahead of him and Troxel's head and shoulders rose out of the sage behind a levelled Winchester. 'I hate to disappoint you, Carmody,' Troxel went on, 'but I figured that nigger was up to somethin' when I saw him saddlin' Booth's black this afternoon. I just says to myself, "I'll stroll out and watch what happens, and maybe Booth'll be glad I did." Well, sir, here I am.'

'You should have told Anson right then, Troxel,' Carmody said, 'because you sure ain't goin' to tell him now.' Troxel tried to jump aside but he had come too close and when Carmody dug spurs to the black the man went down, struggling frantically to escape the flashing hoofs. He failed, and the sodden snap of the man's backbone as the horse went over him told Carmody he would have no need for the drawn Colt now in his hand.

A sudden cry brought Carmody's head around and he saw a rider emerging from the cookshack pointing in his direction and yelling something. Half a dozen others appeared, pouring from the door into the yard, looking for the cause of the excitement. They followed the first man's pointing finger, then broke and ran for their horses.

CHAPTER 13

The course Carmody had chosen for himself lay at a tangent to the sprawling circle of Anvil outbuildings. Now that his escape had been discovered there was danger of his being cut off. Without slackening speed he took in the surrounding country with a quick sweep of his eyes. His only alternative he decided immediately would be to cut sharply away from the ranch, plunging deeper into Anvil territory in the hopes of eluding his pursuers in the approaching darkness. But this was their range and those riders would be familiar with every inch of it while he was not. There was little cover in the long barren slopes, and if he stuck to the shallow valleys a sudden turning into a blind canyon or an unexpected encounter with a stretch of drift fence would leave him trapped. He decided to ride it out.

Half a dozen Anvil riders were now mounted and pounding in a close-packed bunch around the cookshack to intercept him before he reached the slope leading out of the valley. He dug his spurs and lashed the black with his rein-ends and felt the bunched muscles beneath him respond in a fresh burst of speed that left the wind singing in his ears. He broke out of the brush in time to see the riders pull up pell-mell in a cloud of dust, finding their way blocked by the slab fence connecting the outbuildings. Except for one man they wheeled in a body and cut back to round the house where there would be nothing between them and Carmody but the open hardpan.

The remaining rider wheeled back, spurring his horse at the fence. Carmody drew his Colt, watching across his shoulder without breaking the black's stride. The horse rose to clear the fence, his rider hunched low on his withers. He brought it up by the head, swaying crazily in the saddle as the horse stumbled sideways – then he was straightening out, heading to intercept Carmody, closing the gap between them on a collision course. There was a dull flash in the twilight as the man fired, but the distance was too great and the bullet kicked up the dust a dozen yards away.

Carmody swept his head around. To his right lay a steep slope climbing up from the valley floor. It would be a labouring climb, bringing the man quickly within gun range from behind. He could not turn back into Anvil territory, he had already decided that. The only course was to plunge ahead as he was now, with the gap between them steadily diminishing. The whip of a bullet past his head brought him around in the saddle. He could see the shadowy outline of the Anvil rider less clearly now in the deepening twilight. The man fired again, orange flame flickering and disappearing. Carmody wrapped the reins around the horn and lifted his Colt, cradling it in the crook of his left elbow to steady it. Man and horse were blurred into one indistinct shadow. He took aim as well as he could and fired.

The shadow broke in two as the horse somersaulted, catapulting the rider into the air. Carmody saw him for a brief instant, legs and arms flying – then he disappeared.

The black's pace slackened a little now and Carmody knew he was off the flat and climbing gently out the valley toward the V in the low hills to the north-west. He glanced ahead. The V was indistinct now and he took a quick bearing on the few scattered evening stars to mark his way, then turned to look back while he reloaded.

Then he thought of something that brought his head

around with a curse. The fence!

Somewhere up there ahead in the darkness those three tough thin strands of wire stretched along the border of Anvil range, blocking his way as effectively as a band of armed horsemen. And, at the speed he would be travelling if he hit it, just as deadly.

The question was – how far?

He racked his brain, trying to remember how far he had ridden from the gap-gate to Anvil headquarters after his gunfight with Hacker and Hallstead. Four or five miles, but he couldn't be sure. And his course now was at an unknown angle lengthening the distance, perhaps by a mile, perhaps more. The point that bothered him was that he couldn't afford to poke along cautiously in the starlight, feeling for the fence when it might yet be a mile or two away. The men behind would know its position to a yard and would not slacken pace until they came to it or caught up with him. His present lead was, then, only a temporary thing.

With luck, as the starlight brightened and his eyes adjusted to it, he might see the fence sufficiently in advance to slow down. Crossing it would be only a matter of minutes to kick out the staples and tramp the wire down while he led the black across. But first he had to find the fence. And if he should come upon it against the shadow of a hill or in broken country or brush – then he would cut the black to ribbons and probably break his own neck before he could notice the fence was there.

He covered another mile or two without slackening speed, the feeling of apprehension growing within him. He was well out of the valley now and riding through the shallow V in the gently rolling hills. The country here was flatter, and that was to his advantage – except that he remembered that where it bordered Anne's place the ridge was generally broken and cut by gullies along the slope. But that gave him something to go by.

He crossed a ridge and the black veered sharply almost unseating him. A black opening yawned beside him in the starlight, widening as it dropped down the slope. For the first time Carmody reined and let the horse blow while his eyes followed the shallow gully the black had swerved to avoid. Then he saw it, standing faint in the starlight not a dozen yards ahead. A fencepost. He shifted his gaze and found another, and a feeling of elation surged through him. Then he thought of what would have happened if the black had not swerved and the feeling gave way to a small shiver that chased down his spine. He eased the black forward and dismounted.

The staples, he found, were inside, facing Anvil range. He braced his boot against the post and took the top wire in his hands and gave a mighty heave. The wire creaked, then the staple suddenly gave and hit him sharply in the chest. He repeated the process twice more then held the wires down with his foot and coaxed the horse across. In the clear silence of the night he caught the unmistakable sound of running horses. Still distant, maybe a mile or more, but moving fast. And he still had four, maybe five miles to go. With a quick glance at the stars he mounted and headed the black in a more westerly direction.

The light, when he saw it, seemed too far to his left and for a moment it confused him. Then he remembered that he had worked well northward during his ride and had come out well down the valley from the Merriweather ranch. He turned the black and plunged down the long slope toward the line of cottonwoods along the creek. Just before he reached them a shadow crossed the lamplight for an instant, and then the light went out. They had heard him coming.

He hit the creek in a cascade of flying spray and wheeled across the flat when the full meaning of the darkened house struck him and he reined to a skidding halt. He opened his mouth to yell when the hardpan beside him geysered a shower of earth and sand and he ducked involuntarily. The boom of a heavy Sharp's followed on the whine of the riccochet and he found his lungs and bellowed, 'Carmody here! Hey, Caleb, hold it!'

A figure detached itself from the shadow of a cottonwood in the front yard, yelling, 'It's Jeff!' and he recognized Caleb. Spurring the lathered black toward the house Carmody threw a glance over his shoulder. Along the ridge at the top of the valley a scattered dozen dots moved swiftly down the slope in the starlight. Carmody slid from the saddle before the black had stopped and hit the ground in a run.

'Stay in the house!' he warned, plunging through the gate. There was a strange wagon standing in the yard he noticed vaguely and he wondered if that meant Anne had been getting ready to move. Then they were gathering around him in the shadows; Caleb and Anne and Will Henstridge and a woman Carmody guessed must be Will's wife.

He stumbled against the side of the porch and leaned there, catching deep gulps of air and the pain in his chest told him what the ride had cost him. Anne was beside him, her arms about him, her face peering anxiously up at his in the faint light. 'Jeff! – Jeff, are you all right? There's blood on your shirt – what's happened?'

Carmody gestured toward the slope. 'Anson's crew' – he breathed heavily – 'coming to burn you out ... better get inside. I'll tell you about it.'

Will Henstridge was running toward his wagon saying something about going to get his rifle. Carmody herded the others inside, describing briefly what had happened, interrupting himself to ask, 'Ammunition and water? We'll need plenty of both!'

Anne ran to a cupboard and jerked open a drawer, bringing forth several boxes of cartridges. She pointed to the pump at the sink in the corner. 'Clint and Caleb built the house around the well – we've got plenty of water.'

Will Henstridge came running back with his Winchester,

glancing over his shoulder. 'Can't see 'em now – they're scattered along the flat and the trees are in the way.'

'They'll sneak up now and try to fire the place,' Carmody warned. 'They're brought coal oil.' He glanced at the doors leading off the kitchen. 'You ladies had better hunker down behind the stove where it's safe,' Carmody snapped. 'Henstridge, you go in there and watch that side of the house' – he pointed to the parlour – 'and Caleb maybe you'd better take the bedroom.'

Anne had taken her Winchester from the rack and was busy slipping extra cartridges to fill the magazine. She glanced up and said sharply, 'I will not hide behind any stove! This is my ranch and if I can't. . . .'

Carmody grinned at her across the darkness of the kitchen. 'All right, Anne, then maybe you'd better. . . .'

'Oh my God!' Anne breathed as the door behind Carmody opened.

He turned to see Penelope standing there uncertainly in the dimness.

'Who put out the light, Mommy?' Then she saw Carmody and ran to him, grabbing his knees and laughing. 'I knew you'd come back, Jeff! I knew you would!'

From the kitchen window Caleb's heavy Sharp's boomed authoritatively, making everybody jump. 'Damn . . . missed him!' he swore, throwing open the breech and inserting a fresh cartridge. An answering shot showered the room with glass and he flattened against the wall, muttering, 'I seen you – just behind that tall cottonwood. All right, feller, just try it again!'

Will Henstridge grabbed the bucket of water and his Winchester, running toward the parlour. 'Emma! You come on in here – there're two windows and you can take my pistol and cover one.'

Penelope clutched Carmody's knees. 'Jeff, I'm scared! Will they hurt us?'

'No, little lady,' he said firmly. 'They won't hurt us.'

Carmody said softly to her, 'This might last a while, Anne. Maybe we'd better make a bed for her under the table. 'I'll bring the mattress off her cot and put it there; then I'll go in and watch from the bedroom. I can cover the back of the barn from there. That's the side they'll use if they try to. . . .' He stopped, remembering Penelope.

He saw Anne nod. 'All right, Jeff, that's a good idea.'

'If you're going to stay in the bedroom, Jeff, I want to, too!' the little girl said. 'I want to be where you are.'

He glanced at Anne for confirmation and saw her nod her head again. 'I'll feel better if she's with you, Jeff. You can put her mattress on the floor. So she won't be . . . you know.'

'All right,' Carmody said.

'Where's Pinto?' Carmody said softly as he dragged the mattress onto the floor.

Penelope giggled and pointed to a ball of fur in a box in the corner.

'Good watchdog,' Carmody said.

'He's awful tired,' Penelope said defensively. 'He's spent most of the day trying to dig up the coyote Caleb buried.' She giggled again, 'And I 'spect Caleb's almost as tired trying to keep him from it. But' – she hesitated, then said conspiratorily – 'he did dig up something. If you promise you won't tell I'll let you see them. Promise?'

But Carmody was watching the window now and said absently, 'Sure, I promise. But lay down there and go to sleep now.'

A voice called suddenly from beyond the barn and Carmody ran to the window. 'Hallo there in the house! Mrs Merriweather, all we're after is Carmody. Turn him over to us and we'll go away and leave you in peace!'

'In pieces, he means,' he heard Caleb mutter from the kitchen. Then the night shook to the roar of the buffalo gun and the old man taunted, 'Come on in and git him! What the hell's ailin' you?'

'Caleb!' Anne said. 'There're ladies present!'

'Damn – I forgot!' Caleb chuckled, and Carmody could hear the click of the breech as he replaced the spent cartridge.

A long and uneasy silence followed. Carmody could feel the tension building up. 'Get ready,' he said, just loud enough for everyone to hear. 'They'll probably try a rush after that.' He risked a quick trip across the room to glance out of the window on the other side and looked across at the wing where Henstridge and his wife were.

'I'm sorry I got you folks into this,' Carmody called across.

'Hell, that's all right, fella!' was Will's quick reply. 'Ain't your fault.'

Carmody grinned and returned to the other window. He had just reached it when Caleb yelled, 'Here they come!'

The words were almost drowned in the fusilade which followed. The house rattled under the hail of bullets.

The shooting kept up at a rapid pace, the heavy booming of Caleb's heavy Sharp's dominating the return fire from the house. Carmody had not so much as fired a shot; he was too intent on ferreting out the reasoning behind the barrage of pistols and rifles. There had been no bodily rush of men – Anson wasn't chancing that until he found out the positions and numbers of the defenders. He had probably noticed the Henstridge wagon in the yard and knew he would have to deal with more than he had counted on.

But what struck Carmody most was that, so far, the Anvil attack seemed to be coming mainly from the vicinity of the barn. No attempt had been made to encircle the house. Either that meant that Anson was afraid to risk his men away from the safety of the barn itself – or that he was trying to distract the attention of the defenders away from something that was happening elsewhere. Knowing that Anson would have little conscience about the safety of his riders, Carmody bet heavily on the other alternative.

The scathing fire from the barn continued undiminished and the kitchen was filled with the whine of bullets and crash of broken glass and crockery.

'Jeff! Will!' Caleb yelled excitedly, slamming a fresh cartridge home. 'Lend us a hand out here, will you? They're all in the barn and raisin' hell with us out here!'

'Hold it, Will!' Carmody barked. 'Stay right where you are. Caleb, an old Injun scrapper like you ought to know better'n that! That's just what Anson wants – and when he's got us all out there he'll send somebody sneakin' around this side to try and fire the house.'

'Well – mebbe you're right,' Caleb said grumpily. 'But I don't know why the hell it had to be me out here. These walls're about as thick as paper when it comes to stoppin' a bullet.' A loud crash interrupted him as a bullet swept into the kitchen table-high, scattering fragments of the supper dishes across the floor. 'See that!' Caleb yelped, crouching beneath the sill, his eyes searching the darkness for the offending marksman. 'There he is!' he growled in a hoarse whisper. 'Hidin' behind Will's wagon. Watch me nail him!'

'Make damn sure you hit him and not the wagon,' Will called quietly with mock seriousness. 'That damn elephant gun of yours. . . .' He was cut off by the thunderous roar of the Sharps which was followed instantly by the loud clang of iron as the big slug tore into a hub of a wheel at the axle. Craning his neck around the corner of the window Carmody saw the wagon settle with a crash on the broken wheel as a figure detached itself from he wreck and scurried for the cover of the barn. Anne's rifle cracked from the kitchen and the running figure pitched forward, rolling over, and lay still, a dark blot against the lighter background of the yard.

There was a sudden cessation of firing from the barn and in the heavy silence that followed he could hear Anne's voice say tonelessly, 'I-I've killed him!' He knew the shock she must be experiencing at the realization that she had ended a human life, and even though she had done so justifiably in defence of her home and her child the shock would still be there.

Then Will Henstridge's voice spoke up quietly and broke the tension. 'Hell, that's all right, Anne – just lookit what Caleb's done to my *wagon*.'

He heard her give a laugh of sheer relief, but he knew it had bordered closely on hysteria and if Will's odd humour had not intervened it might have been serious. But the moment had passed and he knew it would not return.

As if with sudden angry desire to avenge the dead man, the firing broke loose again more heavily than before. The rattle and whine of bullets and little crashing noises filled the house once more. Something in the darkness outside caught Carmody's attention. Peering cautiously over the sill beside his Colt he moved his eyes slowly over the dark shapes of brush scattered beyond the house at the back. Then he saw it again, beside the henhouse, a form almost indistinguishable in the shadows. It moved as he watched, creeping from behind the henhouse and darting to the shelter of a clump of brush closer to the house. The movement was quick, giving him no time to take aim in that feeble starlight. But it was enough to let him know his earlier guess had been right. The man had been carrying something as he scurried for cover. A jug of coal oil.

CHAPTER 14

From where Carmody stood, he commanded a view of that part of land beyond the house on the side away from the barn. It was sprinkled with brush and a few scrub willows, and not many yards away was the deeper shadow of the tall cottonwoods where the creek bent close to the house. While it offered little protection from gunfire, it was well suited to the type of skulking the man out there was doing.

He stood for a long time watching for a sign of movement while the gunfire behind him continued. He tried to locate the spot where he had first seen the man but became uneasily aware that he had lost it in the confusing similarity of each straggling clump of brush.

Then he saw the man move. Quickly again, darting from shadow to shadow, not exposing himself sufficiently for accurate shooting at that distance in darkness. Carmody marked the spot well this time, then debated the wisdom of borrowing Anne's rifle for a shot at the brush. He decided against it. A misplaced shot would only warn him that he had been spotted, would make him more cautious. Instead Carmody gave himself over to studying the possible line of the man's approach, trying to figure in advance the path he would choose.

A brief examination of the ground made Carmody a little more confident. Close against the house the brush was nonexistent; for a dozen yards or so beyond that it was sparse enough to provide poor cover. Even if the man bellied down and crawled Indian-style every inch of the way he would have to expose himself sooner or later. He would have to come in and pour the coal oil, then light it. But he would never get that far.

Carmody saw him move again, closer this time and angling toward the house. He moved more slowly, too, as though weighing up his chances for a final approach. Carmody watched the patch of brush for a long time, but the man seemed in no hurry to close.

Then the shadow rose above the brush. Closer now, much closer. So close that Carmody drew his hammer to full cock and raised the Colt. The man went through a peculiar motion that was shadowy and indistinct and Carmody wonderingly held his fire. Then he was gone down behind the brush again. Carmody frowned, puzzling the meaning of this. In the next instant the roof gave a peculiar double thud as something landed solidly on either side of the ridgepole.

Still puzzled, Carmody watched the brush for a sign of further movement. Surely the man hadn't thrown the jug of coal oil on the roof and expected it to break and splatter? He frowned again, growing impatient.

A faint gurgling noise caught his ear in a lull in the shooting and he jerked his head upward to stare at the ceiling. Something dripped from the eaves past the window beside him. The smell was unmistakable. It was coal oil. But – how the hell. . . ?

In a flash Carmody saw what the man had done. He had taken a length of rope and tied a chunk of wood or some other heavy object to one end and the jug of coal oil, loosely corked, to the other. Then he had flung them and, with more luck than skill, had made them straddle the ridge of the roof. The impact had knocked the cork loose from the jug and the coal oil was now running down the roof, saturating it and the side of the house.

'Damn!' Carmody muttered, jerking his attention back to the brush where he had last seen the man. 'But you've still got to put a match to it, son,' he thought. Yet the annoying notion stirred in his mind that maybe the arsonist had figured out something for that, too. A bullet, maybe. No, he doubted if a bullet would create enough friction to set off coal oil. You sometimes even had to hold a match a while to get it to catch oil. Then maybe. . . .

A flicker of light appeared suddenly in the brush, then it grew quickly brighter, lighting the whole of the area clear to the cottonwoods along the creek. The man rose above the brush and Carmody saw that he was drawing back his arm to hurl a torch made of a length of stovewood wrapped at one end with rags now blazing furiously from the coal oil in which they had been soaked. Carmody fired twice in rapid succession.

Both shots struck home, staggering the man backward under their impact. The arm holding the torch aloft relaxed its grip and the torch fell, striking the man on the shoulder. The man's clothes were instantly aflame and with a scream of agony he turned and stumbled drunkenly toward the trees, slapping feebly at the flames which enveloped him. The cottonwoods and brush danced crazily in the shifting light as the blazing figure reeled, helplessly, a human torch. A second shuddering scream was cut mercifully short as Carmody sent a third bullet into his back. The man dropped instantly and lay unmoving in a little open space in the brush. For a moment or two the bright flames licked at him, then gradually faded and went out, leaving only a few glowing sparks in the darkness beneath the trees. Carmody turned away from the window and reloaded, his face grim-set. A peculiar sickly-sweetish odour penetrated through the smell of coal oil still dripping slowly from the eaves.

Carmody was conscious of a sudden quiet everywhere. The shooting had stopped. The Anvil men in the barn beyond had either seen or guessed what had happened from the screams and shots. He guessed it was enough to shake even their hardened nerves. Nodding toward the kitchen he said, 'Better get back there, Caleb. No tellin' what they'll try now. I'll be out in a minute.'

The pup was standing there, looking on wonderingly, and Carmody caught him up and held him to Penelope. 'Look, Pinto's here.' She raised her head and glanced at the pup as if it might be the first thing she recognized in all this nightmare. 'You said you'd show me what Pinto dug up this afternoon,' Carmody went on, holding her attention. He felt it was unlikely that Penelope had been seriously affected by what she had witnessed, horrible though it was to see a man burn. He felt it was more a matter of taking her mind off it – hers and Anne's, too.

Penelope looked guiltily at her mother, then reprovingly at him. 'You promised you'd keep it a secret.'

'We'll let your mother in on the secret – just the three of us, huh?'

The girl turned to her mother. 'Will you let me keep them?'

Anne would have let her keep a bear in the parlour right then. 'Of course, Penny. Let's see what they are.'

Penelope turned and drew a box from beneath the wardrobe. Something chinked metallically and she came back holding a pair of spurs. Anne gave a relieved laugh and hugged her to her. 'She's always wanted a pair of her own, Jeff. I was afraid she was too young yet, remembering how I turned into a female wrangler before I was much older I tried to discourage it.' She kissed her little girl and said, 'Of course you can keep them.'

Penelope was overjoyed. She hugged Pinto and thanked him for bringing her the spurs. 'He dug them up when he was looking for the coyote Caleb buried. They must be old – they're kind of rusty and one rowel's missing. But maybe you'll help me fix them up, will you, Jeff?' She held them out to him.

'Can you fix them, Jeff?' Penny said eagerly. 'Can you make a new rowel?'

'Yes, little lady,' he said slowly, his voice strangely thick, 'I think I've got a spare rowel that'll just about fit this. I'll take it along for now. You keep the other.' He shoved the broken spur in his hip pocket. It was too dark to see it plainly. But he felt sure it was the one.

A scattered outburst of shots came from the barn, slamming into the house. Carmody stood up quickly. 'They're starting up again.' He glanced at the kitchen, then out of the bedroom window. 'You'd better stay here with Penny a little longer,' he said. 'I don't think they'll try that again, but you can keep an eye out the window every once in a while. I'm going out in the kitchen and see if I can size up the situation.'

He went quickly through the door, dropping on all fours as a shot slammed into the kitchen, jangling a row of empty tin cans on a shelf.

Carmody said nothing. He slid in beside the window Anne had been guarding and peered over the sill. There was no sign of activity and he expected none. At least not yet. Anson would not try the coal oil stunt again; and it was not in his nature to rush the house. More than likely he would try to sit them out, hoping that lack of water or food would tell on them before many hours passed. He probably did not know about the well in the house.

But water alone would not be sufficient to enable them to hold out forever. Food and ammunition were both essential and the supply of each inside the house was limited. Most of the preserved foodstuffs were stored away in the cellar out beside the henhouse; even the barrels of salted beef had been rolled down there to keep them out of the heat until they had 'set'. Anson, on the other hand, could depend on the creek for water, and a running supply line between here and Anvil could keep the besiegers well supplied with both food and ammunition. There would come a time when the boot would begin to pinch. Maybe in a day; maybe in two or three. But it would come.

Carmody dismissed the worry for the time being. The night was not yet over. The moon would soon rise and that would lessen the danger of a sneak attack. And tomorrow night the moon would rise still later and it might give him a chance to slip away and ride for help.

The thing that concerned him most right now was the knowledge that the old man who crouched beside the opposite window with the Sharp's resting on the sill was the man who had killed Clint Merriweather. The man who had kept his silence and let Carmody spend eight years under shotgun guard behind prison walls.

He shifted his position against the wall and reached for his tobacco, only to find he had none. The movement caused him to feel the pressure of the spur in his hip pocket. Absently his hand moved to his shirt pocket to feel for the rowel he had carried so long – then remembered that it, too, was in the shirt Vicker had taken from him. But it didn't matter. He had seen it often enough in the past eight years to be familiar with every detail of it; to know it matched the one Penelope still had and that it would fit the rowelless spur in his pocket.

He found it strange that now, when he had found the man at last, there was none of the bitterness, none of the hatred he had nursed so long. That had been swept away by the events of the past few days and the realization that life held something more for him that the satisfaction of settling a grudge. Instead the discovery had left him with a feeling of numbed shock, almost of disbelief. He wanted to believe that Dalmas had been right in the first place when he had said that the presence of the lost rowel beside Clint's body had meant nothing. But he knew that was a false hope. The very fact that Caleb had buried the spurs to hide them was an admission of guilt.

'Moon's comin' up,' Caleb said quietly.

Caleb withdrew the Sharp's from the window sill. 'Well, if they come now at least we'll have light to shoot by.' He grinned at Carmody. The grin faded when he saw the way Carmody was staring at him. 'What's the matter, son?' he said anxiously. 'You ain't been hit, have you? You look pretty much all in.'

Carmody nodded slowly. 'I been hit, Caleb. Hit hard.' He pulled the broken spur from his pocket and laid it on the floor between them in the glow of the moonlight.

The old man paused in the act of striking a match, staring at the spur. Slowly he raised his eyes to meet Carmody's. For a long time neither of them spoke. Then Caleb let out a long sigh and his shoulders seemed to droop and he seemed suddenly to age while Carmody watched. 'So – you know,' he said with resignation, his eyes dropping from Carmody's gaze.

'What made you do it, Caleb?' Carmody said with a tinge of bitterness. 'That's what I can't understand – why did you kill him? You told me you'd practically raised him.'

The old eyes met his own and Caleb shook his head. '*Why*, Jeff? I guess there ain't no tellin' why, exactly. Some things that happen in a lifetime can't just be explained away with questions and answers.' His voice grew hoarse and he cleared his throat and glanced anxiously toward the bedroom, nodding his head. 'Does Anne know?' Carmody shook his head.

Caleb sighed. 'Thank God for that. I don't ever want her to know. Not just on account of me, but account of Clint.'

Carmody frowned, puzzled. 'Why on account of Clint?'

The old man glanced out of the window. 'Yeah, I raised Clint,' he said thoughtfully. 'Raised him like he was my own son. But – I guess it was with him like it is with a lot of things that are close to us in this life; you sometimes overlook the bad spots and think only about the good. It was my fault I guess, in a way. I always knew he was a heller, but with a kid you sort of expect that. Knowin' how I was when I was young I felt I couldn't very well bear down on him too hard. I know, now, that I was wrong. You never cure anythin' bad by lookin' the other way and hopin' it'll go away.'

'Clint was a heller?' Carmody said in some surprise. 'I always heard that folks thought quite a lot of him.'

Caleb smiled briefly. 'Sure they did. Most of 'em felt the same way about him I did. They knew he had a wild streak in him, but they all thought he'd grow out of it.'

In the moonlight Carmody could see the hard bitter lines come into his face as he went on. 'But there come a time I realized I'd let things go a little too far. I said he was a heller – but a likeable one. He was the kind women go like flies to molasses. Seems like the wild streak in a man like Clint just naturally draws a woman even though she knows it might get her into trouble. Well sir – there was a little gal down on the Canadian, a rancher's daughter. Pretty little thing. Brought up real nice, folks were good honest people. I think they was always a little leery of Clint, but they liked him too well to come right out and ask what his intentions was concernin' their Annabelle – until it was too late. One day Clint just stopped visitin' their place and I met the gal's dad in town some time later and he mentioned Clint had stopped comin' and wondered why. A few weeks later they knew why. They found her body on a sandbar in the river.'

Caleb sighed and tried to light his pipe and failed. 'Her folks wasn't the kind to go after Clint for revenge. Some ways it might have been better if they had. Maybe if the old man had come gunnin' for Clint it might've put the fear of God into him. Instead of that these folks just up and left the country. I thought sure that'd straighten Clint out, at least where women was concerned. It did – for a while. But every time a woman smiled at Clint he was off. If he drew them like flies he sure didn't bother to try brushin' them off. Not until he was through with 'em. Next thing he did was take up with a married woman down in Canadian. Her husband got wind of it and told Clint what'd happen if he caught him around there again. Clint shied off her for awhile, but there was always plenty of women within a day or two's ride to keep him busy. I packed him off up to Wyomin' on a horse-buyin' trip to get him away from her for a while. It was up there he met Anne. Swept her off her feet, married her – 'cause that's the only way he could get her – and brought her back. Well, I think the whole of Hemphill County breathed a sigh of relief when Clint got married. I know I did. Everybody thought he'd settle down now for good.'

'But he didn't,' Carmody said, beginning to see the pattern now.

Caleb nodded. 'That's right – he didn't. Oh, for a while. Till the newness kind of wore off bein' married to Anne. Then I found out he'd taken up with this married woman down in Canadian again. That was about the time Anne was ready to have her baby. I made her go back East to my sister to have it.'

Caleb turned his head and looked into Clint's eyes. 'You see, Jeff – if I loved Clint like a son, I reckon I growed to love her like a daughter. Only maybe more so because she was at his mercy – like every woman who'd ever met him. This time I felt it was my responsibility to look after her because it was partly my fault Clint was the way he was.' He drew a deep breath and went on. 'Well, anyway – I had some long talks with Clint after she'd gone. Tried to put some sense into his head. But it was too late. He told me to mind my own damn business and stay out of his life.'

Carmody saw the pained look in the old eyes as Caleb ducked his head and brushed his eye angrily with a gnarled forefinger. 'That really hurt, Jeff – comin' from somebody I'd raised from a yearlin'.'

'Well, that night – you know the one I mean – Clint rode out without sayin' anythin' to me. It was early afternoon when he left, and I figured he was off to Canadian to see this woman. Well, I saddled and lit out, takin' a short cut to get there ahead

of him. I went to her and told her what was happenin' and told
her plain to stay away from him from now on. She just laughed
at me. I come ridin' back as fast as I could and caught up with
him on the old stage road. I reckon you know where – you
come along not long after.'

Caleb paused again, as though digging back in his memory,
trying to shape up just how it had happened. 'I don't know
exactly what come over me that night. It's hard to explain to a
stranger how you feel when you see somebody turn against you
who's almost a part of yourself. I told him what I'd done and I
begged and pleaded with him to leave the woman alone and
settle down before he ruined his own life and mine and – and
Anne's and the baby's. Well – he called me a lot of names I've
never took from any man. Said I was an interferin' old goat
and he was tired of grubstakin' me and if I didn't stop
meddlin' in his affairs he'd shoot me. He had his gun out
when he said it and he was plenty mad. Well – I could've stood
all that, I reckon; if it hadn't been for what he said about
Anne. He said she was just another woman as far as he was
concerned, and if she didn't like livin' with him the way he
was, then there was plenty of women who would and she could
go plain to hell.

'Right then I knew – I knew there'd never be an end to it. I
knew a lot of things about Clint I'd never known before. I
knew he'd make Anne's life a misery and enjoy doing it. I-I
guess I just kind of went out of my head. Like I say, he had his
gun out. But I don't think he expected me to draw mine. I
think he was too stunned to know what was happenin'. I know
I didn't believe it myself till it was all over and he was lyin'
there in the road. I got scared then and was so weak and
trembly at the thought I'd killed him that I could barely drag
myself out of the saddle. My right spur caught in a saddle
string when I swung my leg over. The rowel pin was about wore
through – I'd noticed it before and meant to fix it – and I
guess when I tugged loose it broke and the rowel fell off where

you found it.

'I took one look at Clint and knew he was dead. Then I heard your horse comin' and I lit out.'

Carmody sat very quiet. Caleb raised his face to look at him. The old man's voice almost broke as he went on. 'I knew they'd pinned it on you, Jeff. And the Good Lord knows the hell I went through the day of your trial. I kept thinkin' I ought to give myself up – then I knew that if I did the whole thing would come out in the open and Anne would know what kind of a man Clint really was. When the judge gave you only ten years – well, I figured you was young and that ten years out of your life wasn't nothin' compared to what it would do to Anne's if the truth came out.'

Carmody sat for a long time when Caleb had finished. He picked up the spur and turned it over in his hand without even seeing it.

'Well!' Caleb said suddenly. 'You came here lookin' for a man. You've found him. You got a gun – use it!'

Carmody laid the spur aside and slowly shook his head. 'You ain't the man I was lookin' for, Caleb. The man I was lookin' for don't even exist any more. And – as for me havin' spent eight years in prison on account of what happened' – he glanced toward the bedroom – 'I'd do it all over again if it meant her happiness.'

Will Henstridge's voice broke suddenly through the stillness in a cry of alarm. 'Look at the barn! It's on fire – they're burning the barn!'

CHAPTER 15

Carmody jumped to the window. The fire had been started on the far side, away from the house, but already the yellow tongues of racing flames could be seen clearly between the planks. Sparks rushed skyward in the windless air, smoke billowed in a great white loud that blanked out the moon. In a matter of minutes the whole barn was aflame, crackling and roaring as the fire raced over the dry timber. The heat of it was fierce inside the kitchen and Carmody's first agonizing thought was of the coal oil soaked roof over the bedroom. If that caught. . . .

A series of whinnying screams shivered through the firelit night and there was the sound of breaking wood as the trapped animals in the barn fought in vain to free themselves from their stalls.

From the doorway behind him Carmody heard Anne scream. 'The horses! Will – your team's in there too! Oh, the beasts – why didn't they turn the horses loose first!' She ran to the kitchen door and flung it open and stood in full view of the firelight and shouted, 'Turn those horses loose! What kind of men are you to burn helpless. . . .'

Carmody flung himself across the kitchen and caught her around the waist, jerking her inside just as a bullet slammed into the doorjamb. He flung her roughly against the wall and shook her. 'Don't do anything like that again!' he said angrily.

'Do you hear me, Anne?'

She nodded resignedly, sobbing. 'The horses,' she said again, feebly.

'You can get more horses, dammit! It's you I'm worried about. They almost killed you – do you realize that?'

Anne straightened, brushing back a stray lock of hair. 'Sorry, Jeff – I lost my head for a minute I guess.'

A rifle cracked twice in the other room and Will yelled, 'Somebody runnin' around the other side of the house! Emma! Can you see. . . .'

Carmody heard Penelope's scream and was running for the bedroom, jerking out his Colt. In the reflected firelight he saw a man throw one leg over the windowsill, then bring up his gun when he saw Carmody. Both guns exploded together and Penelope screamed again. The man in the window was jerked backward and Carmody heard him hit the ground outside. He ran to the window and looked down. The flickering light showed the face of the kid, Peabody, twisted in an awful grimace, blood oozing slowly from a finger-sized blue hole in his forehead.

'You just couldn't wait, could you kid?' Carmody murmured as he withdrew his head from the window.

Penelope looked at him in a mixture of fright and awe. 'You – you got him, didn't you, Jeff?' she said with pathetic bravery. He put his arm around her and patted her head. 'It was him or us, little lady,' he said quietly.

'Carmody!'

Carmody stood up at the sound of Anson's voice shouting from somewhere in the brush.

'Carmody!' the voice called again, rising on a note of anger.

'Yeah, Anson? I'm here.'

'Come walkin' out with your hands up and we'll let everybody else alone!'

Carmody glanced at the others in the room. Anne's face was strained as she met his glance. She shook her head in pantomime. Caleb's eyes wrinkled in distaste at the thoughts he read in Carmody's own. 'Don't you believe him, son. He came here to wipe us out. You think he'd let us live to tell what he's done here tonight?'

'He's right, Carmody!' Will shouted from the other room. 'Don't be a damn fool. He'll only kill you.'

'Maybe there's some way I could trip him up if I went out there,' Carmody said, thinking aloud. 'Maybe I could get the drop on him somehow and. . . .'

'The only trippin' and droppin' you'd do would be to trip over a bullet and drop down dead,' Caleb cut in. 'Rest easy, son. The moon's up now and it'll last till dawn. He ain't likely to rush us while we can see to shoot. And come daylight we'll be able to pick 'em off one at a time.'

They heard Anson yell again. 'Carmody! You comin' out? Or do you want them womenfolk to burn?'

Carmody was peering around the edge of the window, trying to locate the direction of the voice. 'Where would you say he is, Caleb?'

'Sounds like he's in the bunkhouse. I think I can see somethin' in the window just by the door, but I ain't sure.'

Carmody looked. The bunkhouse window was in deep shadow. He thought he could see something, but he wasn't sure, either. He said quietly, 'Anne, got your Winchester handy?'

Anne put it in his hands and he took it without taking his eyes from the bunkhouse. Moving back a step from the window he knelt down, resting the muzzle on the sill. Firelight played tricks on the sights. The distant window was indistinct, a moving blur. He thought he saw something move and pulled the trigger.

There was a bellow of rage from Anson and he knew he had missed. 'All right, Carmody! If that's the way you want it! Let 'em have it, boys – he's in the kitchen.'

Carmody levered another shot at the bunkhouse and

yelled, 'Get down, Anne!' and dropped his head below the window as the outbuildings erupted in a burst of gunfire, pinpoints of light flicking in a dozen places.

Just then the barn collapsed. The sagging timbers of the loft gave way under the weight of the blazing coal that had been five tons of hay, the roof supports buckled, hung for an instant, then plunged with a roar into the holocaust below. For a moment everything was hidden in an immense cloud of smoke as the packed hay broke open, smouldering. Then the smoke exploded in a column of flame, showering sparks high into the moonlit air. The shooting stopped as even the Anvil gunmen paused to gaze.

Pinto struggled in Penelope's arms, barking wildly, then tore himself loose and bounded for the window sill where he hung for a second half-in and half-out, toenails clawing for a foothold. Then he tumbled out into the yard and ran, zig-zagging, barking crazily at the blazing pile of wreckage.

'*Pinto!*' Penelope screamed as bullets began geysering the earth around the pup, sending him darting hither and thither with renewed excitement. Then he gave a yelp of agony as a bullet slammed into him, sending him tumbling over and over. He got up on his forefeet, crying in pitiful yelps as he dragged his twisted hindquarters, floundering helplessly in circles.

With a shriek Penelope burst out of the door and across the porch into the yard, a tiny running figure in a white nightgown that glowed pink in the light of the flames. She ran toward the stricken pup, heedless of the bullets kicking up the yard around her.

'Come out, Carmody, or we'll kill her!' Anson screamed maniacally.

Carmody had not seen her go; could not see her now because the corner of the house cut off his view. He whirled away from the window in time to see Caleb halfway across the yard. Caleb was waving his arms and screaming at the men in the outbuildings, 'Stop shooting you crazy fools! *She's only a little girl!*'

Penelope was trying to pick up Pinto, but the pain-crazed pup snapped at her and tried to drag himself away. Caleb reached her and was bending to pick her up when he stiffened suddenly and took a staggering step backwards, a look of dumb surprise on his face. Then he went forward, groggily, picked up the girl in his arms. She struggled, kicking screaming '*Pinto! Pinto!*'

Carmody was racing across the yard when Caleb went down, Penelope still struggling in his arms.

'There's Carmody!' Anson shrieked with wild glee. 'Nail him, goddammit, *nail him!*'

Carmody did not hear him. He did not hear the snap and whine of bullets suddenly increase around him. He was only vaguely aware that the ground occasionally moved and jerked in little puffs and jets and that something tugged briefly at his sleeve and then let go. He bent swiftly and picked up Caleb's withered body and draped it over one shoulder. Then he caught Penelope in his arms and turned and stumbled toward the house with his double burden. The house seemed a mile away, and the ground before him was alive with moving jets of earth. Although he was running his legs seemed imbedded in thick mud, his movements dreamlike and slow.

A bullet burned a furrow along his cheek and he jerked his head as though a wasp had stung him. Awareness returned and the roar of guns broke suddenly into his consciousness and he felt the warm trickle of blood on his face and on his belly where the wound had opened again.

Then the house was in front of him and he was stumbling up the steps. He crossed the porch and the door opened and he staggered inside. Eager hands took Penelope from him and he felt Will helping him ease Caleb to the floor. He knelt for a moment, getting his breath, aware that Anne was beside him. She touched his shoulder.

'Jeff! You're – you're hurt!'

He shook his head doggedly. 'I ain't hurt.' He looked up. 'Penny? Is she all right?' Then he saw her, clinging to Anne, sobbing quietly. He nodded his satisfaction and smiled wanly.

'Caleb?' Anne whispered, looking hard into Carmody's eyes.

'Don't know,' Carmody said wearily. He laid his hand on the old man's wrist, feeling for the pulse. There was a widening stain on Caleb's shirt. The pulse was only a flutter. He saw Caleb open his eyes.

'Penny?' the old man croaked. Then he saw her with Anne and smiled.

Caleb opened his eyes and shook his head. 'I ain't goin' to make it this time, son. I got too many winters under my hide. Somebody put that chunk of lead in a mighty touchy spot.' He wheezed slightly and turned to Anne. 'Reckon you could bring me a drink of water, Anne?' She nodded and crept toward the bucket beside the pump. Caleb watched till she had gone then turned to Carmody and said, 'She ain't ever to know – the truth. After I'm gone. Understand? It don't make no difference now what happened. It'd only – break her heart.'

'Sure, I understand, Caleb,' Carmody said.

But he knew Caleb didn't hear him. Caleb was dead.

Anne came back with the dipper of water and held it out to Carmody. He took it and laid it aside, looking at her. She gave a little gasp of realization and stared down at Caleb's face. Then she turned away and began to cry quietly.

Carmody got a blanket from the other room and put it over the old man. Then he glanced out of the window. 'Dawn's beginnin' to break, Will. It'll be daylight soon. You and the girls get some sleep. I'll watch 'em for a while. Ain't much danger right now.'

'You're plumb wore out, Jeff,' Will said protestingly. 'Better let me do the watchin' for a while.'

Carmody shook his head and picked up Anne's Winchester.

'I couldn't sleep anyway, Will. But I'd sure admire some of your makin's. I ain't had a smoke in two days.'

Will produced his tobacco and papers and handed them over.

When Henstridge had gone he picked up Caleb's Sharp's and opened the breech. It was loaded. He went through the old man's pockets and found four more shells. These he took and laid them in a row on the floor beside the window. Then he squatted down with the Sharp's in front of him and the Winchester at his elbow and looked out the window at the approaching dawn. And he wondered vaguely if he would ever see another.

It came slowly, first a grey line along the hills to the east, gradually lightening to silver and then changing to pale gold as the sun peered over the rim of the world bathing the Panhandle country in the soft glow.

Beyond the still-smouldering heap of the barn, the out-buildings lay quiet in the early morning stillness. He let his eyes wander slowly among the trees and scattered brush, searching for the Anvil horses. But a company of cavalry could successfully hide their horses within a hundred yards of the house and never show a hair. He wondered vaguely if Anson might have thought, too, about the barn-fire being seen and drawing help. Then he heard a horse whicker somewhere along the creek and knew that Anson was still out there.

He was sitting beside the stove with his back to one wall where it made an angle with another. From this position he could keep a good watch out the near window and the one onto the porch without exposing himself. If anything moved in that entire landscape where the Anvil riders lay he would be sure to see it.

He had finished his cigarette and was leaning forward to stub it out when the wall behind him shook with a thump and he felt plaster powdering its way down his neck. He jerked his head around and saw where a rifle bullet had imbedded itself.

It caused him to shiver a little when he thought that if he hadn't leaned forward to put out the cigarette that bullet would have gone through his head instead of the plaster.

The crack of the rifle followed almost immediately and he realized before he looked out of the window that this shot had not come from the outbuildings or anywhere at ground level. Unless he raised his head high it would be impossible for them to see it. He ran his eyes quickly over the stand of cottonwoods and almost immediately found what he sought. A wisp of gunsmoke floated through the green leaves some fifty feet above the ground. Another puff of white blossomed out as he watched and he threw himself forward on the floor and glanced back in time to see the bullseye pattern in the plaster when the bullet struck. Gathering his feet under him he reached for the Sharp's and pulled the hammer to full cock.

There was an unmistakable glint of sunshine on metal as the man levered a fresh cartridge. It was gone in an instant but Carmody knew now where his target lay. He poked the muzzle of the heavy Sharp's onto the window sill and dropped the sights fine on the spot where the glint had disappeared. The buffalo gun thundered like a small cannon and jammed his shoulder hard.

For a second nothing happened. Carmody squinted through the gunsmoke, breathing the acrid smell of it, his eyes intent on the spot high up in the cottonwood. Then the leaves shook, once – then again lower down, as if something were falling. From the lower branches a figure dropped, cartwheeling arms and legs, and disappeared into the under-growth beneath the tree. The rifle followed, clattering loudly from limb to limb. Carmody reloaded the Sharp's, scanning the other trees carefully. Satisfied they were empty, he leaned the rifle against the wall and sat back.

'Nice shootin',' Will said quietly from the other room.

'That old buffalo gun sure reaches right out there,'

Carmody replied. 'Doubt if I'd've got him with the Winchester.'

Henstridge gave a sudden whoop from the other room. 'Jeff! Looky yonder! Riders a'comin'. Help's a'comin'. Somebody seen the barn on fire. Half a dozen – no, seven – eight!'

Carmody scrambled to his knees. 'You sure it ain't help for *them*?' He peered out of the window. 'Where are they? I can't see anything.'

'Naw, not out there – in here. Comin' from the direction of town.'

Carmody crossed the kitchen in a running crouch, followed by Anne. Will was at the parlour window, pointing. 'See, comin' down the slope.'

'It looks like Mose Dalmas,' Anne said. 'But – who's that man at the back. He looks like a negro!'

Carmody's tired face broke in a grin. 'That's just a boy from Vicksburg lookin' for a railroad ticket home.' Anne and Will gave him a puzzled look but his mind was already on other things and the grin was gone. 'Sure wasn't able to raise much of a posse, was he? Well, maybe that's all to the good. A big crowd would have made a lot of noise.' He leaned out of the window studying the terrain, then he pulled back in and glanced toward the kitchen. 'Chances are they were too far away to hear those last shots,' he said, talking aloud to himself. 'They might figure we're dead and ride right on in to an ambush. But if we fire a few shots they'll catch on.'

'Anson'll run as soon as he sees 'em!' Will said emphatically.

'If Mose had a dozen men, maybe he would. But Anson won't back down while he's still got a chance.' He glanced out the window again. 'And if Mose keeps comin' like he is the house will hide him from Anson until he gets right down on the creek.'

Will looked at him sharply. 'You mean – maybe we can bottle Anson up?'

144

'Maybe. I just hope he didn't hear that war whoop you let out and start lookin' around to see what caused it. If we let Mose get as close to the house as he can without lettin' on he's comin', and then cut loose at Anson with every gun we've got. . . .'

'Then Anson's bound to cut loose right back at us and that'll warn Mose and let him know where Anson is – that what you mean?'

Carmody nodded. 'Somethin' like that. Now look – see that big-boled cottonwood there on the creek? All right, when Mose and his riders get even with that they're close enough. Then you start shootin'. As soon as I hear you I'll open up, too. Use your pistol in one hand and your rifle in the other. Don't matter a damn whether you hit anythin' or not – but if you can pick one off, so much the better. But the idea is to get Anson's attention so's he won't be likely to notice Dalmas until it's too late. Make him think we've got a whole damn army in here when we cut loose.'

Will chuckled. 'All right, by damn, I'll bet you Emma and me can make more noise in here than you and Anne can make out there. How many guns have we got all told?'

'Well, let's see,' Carmody said. 'Three rifles, to start with. And – yeah – three handguns, yours, mine and Caleb's.'

'Four,' Anne put in. 'I've still got Clint's.'

'Seven altogether. Anne, you take Clint's pistol and your Winchester. Rest the barrel on the windowsill and you can pull the lever down without having to lay the Colt aside each time. Will, you can do the same. Emma can handle Caleb's pistol. I'll take the Sharp's and my own handgun.'

Will nodded, glancing out of the window. 'They're down on the flat now, Jeff. I'll have to keep my eyes peeled to see 'em through the trees.'

'All right. We'll go back in the kitchen and get set. Remember – as soon as they get even with that big cottonwood.'

Anne went to waken Emma and tell her the plan while Carmody crouched beneath the kitchen window and began checking the guns and laying out spare ammunition where it would be handy. There wasn't much, but it didn't matter a lot now. As long as he remembered to hold back six rounds for his own Colt. That was for Anson.

Emma Henstridge went in to join her husband and Anne came back into the kitchen and took her station by the window opposite Carmody. She checked her guns, then smiled over at him. 'Scared?' he asked.

She shook her head vigorously till her hair bounced and glinted golden lights in the sunshine. Impulsively, Carmody leaned over and drew her to him and kissed her. When they drew apart she ran her finger gently along his cheek beside the bullet wound. 'Does it hurt much, Jeff?' she whispered.

'Not much.' Then he grinned. 'But I probably won't be able to shave for our weddin'. Do you mind?'

'Jeff, honey – I wouldn't mind if you had whiskers four feet long!'

CHAPTER 16

Carmody had timed it well. The burst of gunfire from the house came just as Mose Dalmas and his posse swung past the big-boled cottonwood at a lope and forded the creek. The riders wheeled into view just as the Anvil crew opened up from the outbuildings with a barrage that rattled against the walls of the house like a sudden summer hail-storm. For an instant Dalmas wheeled in, hesitating, his blood running cold with fear at the realization that Anvil was in command of the situation. But only for an instant – then something that had lain dormant in his nature for years, some better part of him that had been gradually cowed by the growing power of Booth Anson, came surging up within him and he became a lawman once again instead of a frightened and uncertain man who wore a star and looked the other way when trouble showed.

With a loud yell and a sweep of his arm he led his riders to encircle the outbuilding and cut off possible escape. They rode past at a furious clip, bending low over their horses' necks and firing at the Anvil crew as they passed. Even Wash, frightened though he was and ungainly on horseback, followed in their wake brandishing a muzzle-loading shotgun he had unearthed somewhere on Anvil before riding for help.

The sudden fury of the gunfire from the house plus the unexpected appearance of the sheriff and his posse had an effect on the Anvil crew much like that of a charge of buckshot emptied pointblank into a brushpile full of rabbits. They scampered out of the outbuildings and headed for the brush where their mounts were waiting, running low and keeping the buildings between themselves and the fast-riding posse. One man was cut off from the rest, trapped by an angle of the corral fence and an adjoining shed. He bellied low in the dust while the posse galloped past without seeing him. Then he jumped up and started to run when the straggling Wash on a weary grey mare came lumbering around the corner of the corral at a clumsy gallop. The Anvil man flattened himself against the shed and raised his Colt, waiting for Wash to come in line.

From the house Carmody saw only the shadow of the man against the shed as he raised the pistol. 'Wash! Look out!' he bellowed.

Wash jerked his head, his eyes wide with terror as he saw the gunman not ten feet away levelling his pistol. The ancient shotgun rested across Wash's saddle, fully cocked, but his arms refused to function when he tried to raise it. He closed his eyes and muttered a prayer, pressing the stock against his belly and pulling both triggers simultaneously.

Carmody heard the double blast and saw the cloud of smoke envelop horse and rider. The Anvil gunman toppled forward, a pulpy mass above his shirt collar where his head had been. Wash reappeared through the smoke minus the shotgun, clinging hard to the horn as the old mare put on a surprising burst of speed and clutching his belly where the shotgun had kicked him unmercifully. The mare thundered into the cottonwoods and disappeared. Carmody and Will Henstridge let out a whoop of laughter and then swung their rifles to bear on a pair of Anvil riders who had mounted in the brush and were swinging wide to cross the creek in an attempt to reach the slope beyond. Both shots blended in a single report. The lead rider jerked from the saddle and hit the ground, rolling over twice in the sand before coming to rest with one outstretched arm in the running water of the creek. The second swayed crazily, turned and fired at the house, then doubled slowly forward and slipped from the saddle as his horse hit the creek in a fountain of spray. When the horse reappeared on the other bank the man was hanging by a foot from one stirrup, his body bounding and jerking with each stride of the running mount.

The firing dwindled to a few spasmodic shots, then suddenly ceased. In the deafening silence that followed, Carmody heard a woodpecker drumming a distant tree and somewhere up the valley slope a calf bawled after its mother. The quiet peacefulness of the sounds seemed strangely out of place in the harsh sunlight where smoke still rose from the embers of the barn and men lay sprawled in the grotesque gestures of death.

Will Henstridge broke the silence, saying quietly from the other room, 'Jeff, what d'you reckon got into Mose Dalmas all of a sudden? Why, he acted like a sheriff.'

'Might've been somethin' he et for breakfast,' Carmody said with a weary grin.

'Well, by granny, if he makes a steady diet of it he just might get himself elected again. Lookit there – here he comes with what's left of the Anvil crew. Three . . . four, six . . . seven.'

Carmody stood up and swung a leg over the windowsill, squinting in the sunlight toward the brush from which Dalmas and his posse were herding the cowed Anvil gunmen. 'I don't see him,' Carmody said thinly, his pulse quickening. 'Do you see him, Will?'

'You mean Anson? No – come to think of it, I ain't seen him. Do you reckon he's still in there in the bunkh—'

Some sixth sense had already warned Carmody and his eyes were swinging toward the bunkhouse when he saw the movement by the distant window and shoved himself backwards into the kitchen. The bullet whispered hotly as it passed him, clanged against the handle of the frying pan on the stove and sent it spinning across the room.

'I should've known better,' Carmody said quietly, picking himself up from the floor. He edged to the window and yelled, 'Dalmas! Watch out for Anson! He's in the bunkhouse.'

Anson shouted something and a second shot tore angrily through the window beside Carmody. He moved his head back quickly and grinned at Anne. 'I think he's mad at somebody.'

Anne didn't return his smile but peered cautiously out of her window and said anxiously, 'Jeff – look at Mose Dalmas. He's riding straight up to the bunkhouse.'

Carmody looked. 'Why the damned old fool!' he said, but there was more admiration than censure in his tone and he added softly, 'I've guessed wrong about a few men in my time.' He was thinking of Caleb and Clint Merriweather. 'But I've never guessed as wrong as I have about Mose. He's got iron in him someplace – but that won't keep him from gettin' killed.' He raised his head and yelled, 'Mose! Get back there! You tryin' to commit suicide? Get back – we'll smoke him out of there.'

'I'll handle this, Carmody,' Dalmas shouted belligerently and continued to ride slowly forward.

'Damn fool!' Carmody swore. 'Now he's just tryin' to show us how much spunk he has got. If he'd only wait a minute. . . .'

'That'll do, Dalmas!' Anson called. 'I got you covered. Now get down off that horse and lead him up here.'

The sheriff continued to ride slowly toward the man in the bunkhouse. 'You ain't got a prayer in hell, Booth. I got your crew. I got your horses. I got you surrounded. Now come out of there and give yourself up. If you shoot me you ain't goin' to leave that shack alive and you know it!'

There was abject silence for a while while Anson studied the obvious truth of this statement. Dalmas rode up to within ten feet of the bunkhouse.

'Come on out, Booth. Come out with your hands up and I'll see you get a fair trial.'

'How do I know that?' Anson hedged. 'You're tryin' to arrest me when it's Carmody you ought to be after. He killed three of my men – that's why I came after him. I ain't done nothin' wrong. Carmody's the man you want.'

'I suppose you burned down the barn to see if he was under it.'

'That was an accident. One of the boys knocked over a lantern by accident, that's how the barn burned. You can't arrest me for that. Now what about Carmody? You goin' to let him off scot free after he's murdered three of my men?'

There was a long moment of hesitation in which Carmody murmured to Anne, 'He'll come out. But only because he knows he's a dead gopher if he stays in.'

'All right,' Anson called. 'I'll come out. But you ain't got nothin' on me.

The door opened slowly, then Anson appeared in the doorway, glancing quickly around. Carmody felt a sudden tingle of alarm. 'I don't like this,' he growled. 'I'd better get out there.'

He handed Anne the Winchester and was moving across the kitchen for the door when it happened.

'Throw your gun down!' Dalmas ordered. Anson slid the Colt from his holster, tossed it impudently on the ground beside the sheriff's horse. Dalmas dismounted, pistol in hand, and bent to pick it up. Anson slipped his hand inside his shirt, drew a second Colt from his waistband and shot Dalmas twice in the back.

Carmody was on the porch when he heard Anne's scream a second before the crash of the shots. He bounded into the yard with his gun drawn in time to see Anson lashing Mose's horse into a furious gallop for the trees. He fired twice. Too rapidly. He missed. The third time he steadied, took careful aim, squeezed the trigger. But the range had rapidly lengthened and the shot cut harmlessly through the under-brush as Anson disappeared into the trees.

The posse had turned to look at the sound of the shooting, momentarily bewildered. Carmody yelled what had happened, pointing in the direction Anson had taken. While the possemen ran for their horses he shouted for Will to keep guard on the Anvil crew and ran over to kneel beside Mose.

The examination was brief. Dalmas was dead from two shots in the back, close to the spine. Carmody spun away, running around the bunkhouse to where the captured Anvil horses had been gathered.

Wash was there, holding a pistol uncertainly on the Anvil hands while one of them advanced slowly toward a horse. 'Ah'll shoot!' Wash was saying unconvincingly. 'You tech that hoss, mistuh, an' Ah'll shoot!'

'Go ahead, *shoot*!' the man taunted, laying a hand on the bridle. 'You couldn't hit nothin' anyway, Wash. Shoot!'

Carmody came running up. 'Go ahead and shoot him, Wash,' he called. 'You'll save me the trouble later.'

The man jerked around. 'You can't hold me here, Carmody,' he said angrily. 'You got nothin' on me – it was all Booth's doin', not ours. Just let us have a horse apiece and we'll get out of the country.'

Carmody shoved him aside and mounted the horse. 'Will, hurry up!' he yelled at Henstridge who was running across the yard. 'And if any of these boys try to walk, run or jump, let 'em have it.'

Carmody was crossing the creek now, eyes sweeping the valley and the slope beyond for sight of the riders. He spotted them half a mile away down the valley and swung after them.

Their direction puzzled him. Anson was nowhere in sight. But then he had had a pretty good start and could be anywhere ahead in the maze of canyons and gullies that let into the valley from either side. Either that or they had lost him, and he couldn't believe that. He caught up with them in a side canyon just two miles short of the Anvil fence. As he fell in beside them he yelled to ask where Anson was.

'Somewhere up ahead,' one of them yelled back. 'He's headin' for Indian Territory sure as hell. Once he crosses out of the Panhandle we'll never get him. But – he ain't goin' to get that far,' he added grimly.

Carmody stared ahead, thinking, his eyes running over the ground looking for sign. But the tiny canyon floor was rocky here and left no trail that could be followed except by close and painful scrutiny at a walking pace. He wheeled the bay abruptly away from the others and called, 'I got a hunch he headed back for Anvil. There's a little black box he left there that's he's mighty interested in.'

The others pulled in, staring dubiously at him. 'If it was me,' one of them said, 'I wouldn't hang around for no box. I'd get to hell out of the country the quickest way possible. And the quickest way is to head up into Indian Territory dead east of here. If he was goin' to head for Anvil he'd of cut straight up the slope when he left the Merriweather place.'

Carmody shrugged, said, 'All right. If I find I'm wrong I'll swing back and join up with you. I'll stay with him if I have to track him clear to Arkansas. But I got a hunch I won't have to.' Carmody cut back up the slope and headed for Anvil.

He came out of the canyon onto high ground, saw the Anvil fence on the low, rolling ridge ahead, dipped down into a gully and cut toward it. A few minutes later his heart gave a leap. For a stretch of some thirty yards loose shale showed freshly turned damp where Anson's mount had cut wide, rounding a curve at high speed. His hunch had been right!

The long-legged bay suddenly stumbled, faltered. Carmody glanced down, saw the stream of blood pumping out of the animal's chest. Then the crack of a rifle reached his ears just as the mount buckled and rolled head over heels. At the first sign he had kicked his feet free of the stirrups and levered himself out of the saddle with his hands pushing hard against the pommel.

He hit hard on his shoulders, grateful for the soft shale

along the gully wall. He rolled in a somersault and came up on his knees, tugging out his gun. Shale exploded in his face and he threw an answering shot at the puff of smoke blossoming from the clump of sage on the rim of the gully up ahead. But the range was too far for a handgun and Anson had the advantage of having Dalmas' rifle. The smoke blossomed again and Carmody scrambled for a protecting shoulder of the gully bank as the bullet kicked up the shale where he had been kneeling.

For a good minute while he reloaded Carmody gave vent to his fury until he ran out of words. He stared glumly at the dead horse some twenty feet away and began swearing again. Then he raised his head and listened intently. The sound of fast-fading hoofbeats drifted down the gully and he knew that Anson was gone.

He came out cautiously, knowing it could be a trap, but doubting it because there was little likelihood that Anson would hang around to settle a personal grudge now when he needed every minute of time to put distance behind him. Peering up the gully Carmody saw that the sagebrush now stood clearly etched against the sky. He came out and began to climb laboriously up the side of the gully. He reached the top in time to see Anson remount after passing through the Anvil wire and then disappear over the top of the ridge.

CHAPTER 17

Carmody sighed heavily and started walking along the rim of the gully, back toward the ranch on the creek. With a little luck, he thought glumly, he ought to make it just after dark.

He had covered about a quarter of a mile and had stopped to rest his aching feet, squatting in the shade of a lone juniper, when a sound brought his head up with a jerk. A horseman rounded a bend in the canyon, coming at a dead run. He gave a little cry and stepped out from behind the juniper and raised his arms and yelled. It was Anne.

She dismounted to wait for him while he came slipping and sliding down the shale bank, grinning sheepishly. She ran toward him and hugged him tightly, saying, 'Oh, Jeff! I'm glad I found you – I was scared. Awfully scared. What happened? Where's your horse?'

He told her, briefly, what had happened.

She glanced toward Anvil range for a minute, then said quietly. 'It doesn't matter now, Jeff. He's gone. Maybe the valley can settle down now. It will be nice not to have to worry anymore each time you go to bed whether you might be wakened in the middle of the night by. . . .'

She turned toward him and caught the look on his face. She grabbed his arms and said, 'Jeff – don't! Don't look at me like that. I know what you want to do, but I can't let you. He – he'll kill you! It isn't worth it, Jeff, honestly. . . .'

'I'll borrow your horse, Anne,' he said firmly. 'I'll be back in an hour or so.'

'All right, then, Jeff,' she said quietly. 'I can see you've got to go.' She turned toward the horse. 'You get up first and help me up behind you.'

He stared at her. 'You – you can't go down there! He'll. . . .'

She smiled at him. 'If we're going to be married you might as well get used to me, Jeff.'

Booth Anson skidded his lathered mount to a halt outside the gate and jumped from the saddle into the yard, bounding up the steps and into the house. In his office he knelt beside the safe, cursing its reluctance to open, his fingers shaking with a nervousness. He jerked the door open and seized the japanned box and opened it, unfolding the map hastily to identify it. Then he wadded it up and dug a match from his pocket and lit it, tossing the burning paper into the fireplace. He watched it for a second to make certain it was burning, then returned to the safe and rummaged through it again, taking out three doeskin bags which chinked metallically as he put them down. There was a big brown envelope which he ripped open, glancing inside to make sure he had the right one. He paused to riffle the green bills, smiling faintly. There was close to fifty thousand in cash here. He hated to lose Anvil, but it had cost him nothing but time and fifty thousand wasn't bad profit anyway.

He stood up and jerked a pair of saddle-bags from a peg on the wall, stuffing the envelope and the doeskin bags into the pockets and buckling them shut. Turning, he surveyed the room with a quick glance searching for anything of value that might be small enough to take. Then, as if just remembering something, he darted to the bookcase beside the fireplace and began shoving books aside until he found the bottle of whiskey he had left there.

'To Jeff Carmody,' he said, lifting the bottle. Then as an

156

afterthought he added, 'Damn him.' He drained the bottle and shattered it in the fireplace, then picked up the saddle-bags, wiping his mouth on the back of his hand. The raw whiskey on an empty stomach made him belch and he thought of food. He went through to the kitchen and dropped the saddle-bags on a chair, jerking open the door into the larder-cave below. Not bothering with a lamp he struck a match and held it high. It was cool down here after the heat of the sun, and the whisky glowed in him removing the nervous haste of a few minutes before. There was a certain encouraging solidity in the familiar surroundings, even though he knew he was leaving them for good.

He could feel vibrations now and there was no mistaking their origin. Someone was in the vicinity on horseback. He could feel the hoofbeats plainly. In a bound he was up the steps into the kitchen where he picked up the saddle-bags and raced to the front of the house to look out.

There was no movement anywhere out there. His eyes traversed the long sweep of the valley in both directions clear to the rim. Stepping quickly off the verandah he edged around the house, peering cautiously around each corner before moving round it. A clump of trees partially blocked his view to the north-west, the direction from which trouble would come. He stood for a minute, debating. Whoever it was could still be a long way off.

He ran around to the front where Dalmas' lathered horse stood cropping grass beside the watering trough in the wagon yard. Anson paused just long enough to jerk the rifle from its scabbard, then hurried on to the corral.

Jeff Carmody drew rein behind the clump of trees and peered through the leaves at the house less than a hundred yards ahead. 'Can't see anythin',' he said quietly to Anne behind him. 'But the corrals are on the other side. I reckon he'll be there – if he ain't already gone.' He threw a leg over the pommel and slid to the ground, looking up at her. 'You stay here. I'll be back in a minute.' He said it calmly, as if he might be going to take a stroll.

She reached down and caught his shoulder. 'Jeff!' He glanced up at her again, waiting. 'Jeff – be careful, will you?'

He smiled briefly. 'Sure, I'll be careful. See you in a little while.' Their eyes held for a minute longer, then he turned away and began walking toward the house.

Carmody walked slowly, keeping to the shelter of the trees as much as possible. He came out of the trees very close to the house and stood very quietly, in full view. Then he moved parallel to the fence, keeping well outside it but not too far. His eyes searched the windows on both floors as he went, but he was met by their blank stares of emptiness. Then he saw a horse cropping grass by the water trough in the wagon yard and stopped.

It was Mose Dalmas' horse, he realized. Still saddled, the lather drying in crusty patches on flanks and belly. He shifted his gaze from the horse to the corral beyond. Something moved in the dim interior of the barn beyond the corral and he heard the unmistakeable slap of a saddle being dropped on a horse's back. He pulled at his Colt with his forefinger, letting it slide halfway out before letting it carefully back. Then, with his thumb, he set the hammer at half-cock to reduce the distance he would have to pull it back when the time came. With his eye on the stable door he walked past the gate and across the wagon yard and stood beside the open gate of the corral.

As he waited he noticed a pair of saddle-bags draped over a corral pole near the stable door and he smiled thinly.

The sound of moving hoofs, soft on the litter of the stable floor, came to his ears just an instant before Anson loomed in the doorway leading a horse. Anson started to reach for the saddle-bags, then froze. He had seen Carmody.

Anson straightened slowly, warily, turning to face him.

Their eyes met; Carmody's pale and unmoving like drops of ice, Anson's swinging over the background behind Carmody looking for others.

'It's just me, Booth,' Carmody said quietly. 'I don't need a passel of hired gunmen to back me up.'

Anson felt the friendly glow of the belted whisky strengthening his confidence now that he realized Carmody was alone. The man was a damn fool right to the last with his melodramatic heroics. 'Maybe you'll wish you had, fella,' he grinned. 'I don't hire men because I can't handle a gun. I hire them because it saves me trouble.'

'This is one trouble they won't save you from. I'm waitin' on you to move, Anson. I've got a debt to collect for Caleb and Mose Dalmas and a lot of others.'

Anson glanced at the sun, squinting. 'You're makin' sure you got all the advantage, ain't you, Carmody. Careful to keep the sun at your back so that I can't see you, ain't you?'

'If that's all that's worryin' you,' Carmody said, moving sideways to put the sun between them, 'I'll be glad to oblige by. . . .'

Too late he saw the ruse. He was off balance with one foot awkwardly in front of the other when Anson's hand flashed down and up, glinting in the light. Carmody tried to make up for lost time, keeping his motions to a bare minimum. But the gun seemed to stick in the holster, the hammer seemed welded to the frame. He saw Anson grin and disappear behind a cloud of smoke and knew he was drawing too late.

Overconfidence made Anson over anxious and he fired before the gun was full level and the slug furrowed the ground three feet in front of Carmody showering him with dirt. His own gun was jumping in his hand now though he was not conscious of any sound and was vaguely surprised to see the cloud of gunsmoke blossoming repeatedly from it. Then the smoke parted a little and he saw Anson weaving, his face white and contorted with a look that was a mixture of pain and

159

astonishment, his shirt front a bloody and torn mess. His left hand still clung to the reins of the horse he had led out and the animal was rearing and plunging from the gun noise, Anson swaying jerkily on the reins. Then the man's eyes glassed over, his face lost all expression and seemed to sag. Still gripping the reins he swung under the horse's neck as he fell, his body lifting and falling with each plunge of the horse, his bones crunching sickeningly as the shod hoofs pounded him repeatedly.

Carmody stood transfixed for a split second, then ran forward and caught the reins and pulled the mount aside, talking to it to quieten it. He glanced down at the mangled form on the ground and did not recognize Booth Anson. He turned away.

At the corral gate he leaned heavily against a post, unconscious of the Colt still in his hand. Something moved just on the edge of his vision and he lifted his head. Anne shoved open a side door of the barn and came running toward him, rifle in hand.

'Jeff! Are you all right?' She ran up to him, then stopped a few feet away, her eyes staring at the man behind him on the ground. 'Oh my God!' she whispered, closing her eyes. He went up to her and put his arms around her.

'It's all over, now, Anne,' he said.

Together, slowly, they walked back across the wagon yard.